DOVER·THRIFT·EDITIONS

The Unknown Masterpiece and Other Stories

HONORÉ DE BALZAC

DOVER PUBLICATIONS, INC.
Mineola, New York

DOVER THRIFT EDITIONS

GENERAL EDITOR: PAUL NEGRI
EDITOR OF THIS VOLUME: JOHN BERSETH

Copyright

Copyright © 1999 by Dover Publications, Inc.
All rights reserved under Pan American and International Copyright Conventions.

Published in Canada by General Publishing Company, Ltd., 30 Lesmill Road, Don Mills, Toronto, Ontario.
Published in the United Kingdom by Constable and Company, Ltd., 3 The Lanchesters, 162–164 Fulham Palace Road, London W6 9ER.

Bibliographical Note

This Dover edition, first published in 1999, is a new translation of five stories originally published in French as Le chef-d'oeuvre inconnu, Un épisode sous la Terreur, Facino Cane, Une passion dans le désert, and Le réquisitionnaire. The footnotes and the Note have been specially prepared for this edition.

Library of Congress Cataloging-in-Publication Data

Balzac, Honoré de, 1799–1850.
   [Selections. English. 1999]
   The unknown masterpiece and other stories / Honoré de Balzac.
      p. cm.
   Contents: The unknown masterpiece — An episode during the Terror — Facino Cane — A Passion in the Desert — The Revolutionary Conscript.
   ISBN 0-486-40649-0 (pbk.)
   1. Balzac, Honoré de, 1799–1850—Translations into English. I. Title.
PQ2161.A67   1999
843'.7—DC21
                                        98-49245
                                           CIP

Manufactured in the United States of America
Dover Publications, Inc., 31 East 2nd Street, Mineola, N.Y. 11501

Note

HONORÉ DE BALZAC was born in Tours, France, on May 22, 1799, and moved with his family to Paris in 1814. He was a law clerk from 1817 until 1819 but gave up his chance to become a lawyer in order to follow his literary ambitions. By then his parents had moved away from Paris, but he persuaded them to grant him a small allowance so that he might live in his Parisian garret and write. This he did with great energy but modest success. His plays attracted little notice, but several melodramatic novels that he wrote, generally with hack writers of his acquaintance, were published pseudonymously. His writing failed to provide sufficient money for his extravagant tastes, however, and he decided to go into business. Here, too, success eluded him, first as a publisher of French classic literature and then as owner of a printing shop and a type foundry. By 1829 he was deeply in debt. That same year his novel *Les Chouans* was published, the first book with the name Honoré Balzac on its title page. It sold reasonably well, and from then on the real story of his life is that of his creations, as dozens of remarkable novels and short stories flowed from his pen in almost superhuman abundance. In 1831, with the publication of his popular *La peau de chagrin* (The Wild Ass's Skin), Balzac followed his father's lead in attaching the aristocratic "de" to the family name.

In the mid-1830s Balzac conceived the idea of arranging most of his work into a single unifying cycle that would reflect all the facets of French life. He then began to alter some of his published works to fit them into his grand plan. Some of his characters were renamed, and many of them reappeared from book to book as his themes and theories were played out in various settings. By 1841 he had decided on a title for his work—*La comédie humaine* (The Human Comedy), perhaps echoing Dante's *The Divine Comedy*. Generally, 92 works are counted in this grand cycle, which is divided into three parts: Studies of Manners, Analytic Studies, and Philosophic Studies. The longest division, Studies of Manners, is subdivided into six sets of "Scenes": Private Life, Political Life, Parisian Life, Military Life, Provincial Life, and Country Life. The best-known works in the cycle are the novels *Eugénie Grandet* (1833), *Le père Goriot* (1834; Old Goriot), and *La cousine Bette* (1846). A notable work that is not in the cycle is *Contes drolatiques* (1832; Droll Stories), a collection of 30 ribald stories told in the manner of a medieval storyteller like Rabelais.

Although Balzac may have organized his writings in neat compartments, his personal life was often in chaos. His popular success brought substantial earnings, but he was often forced to flee debt collectors. As much as he loved luxury and extravagance, Balzac loved women even more. Complications and confrontations were commonplace, as were the inspirations and insights he gained from his *amours*. He finally married the one true love of his life, a Polish countess named Evelina Hanska, in 1850. Unfortunately, by then his health was failing. He died August 18, 1850, age 51. Unlike a host of long-forgotten writers, Balzac never received France's highest literary honor, membership in the Académie Française. Today his work lives on in numerous editions published in many languages.

Contents

THE UNKNOWN MASTERPIECE

TO A LORD. 1845.

1. Gillette

TOWARD THE END of the year 1612, on a cold December morning, a young man whose clothing looked very thin was walking to and fro in front of the door to a house located on the Rue des Grands-Augustins in Paris. After walking on that street for quite some time with the indecision of a lover who lacks the courage to visit his first mistress, no matter how easy her virtue, he finally crossed the threshold of that door and asked whether Master François Pourbus was at home. On the affirmative reply made by an old woman busy sweeping a low-ceilinged room, the young man slowly climbed the steps, stopping from stair to stair like some recently appointed courtier worried about how the king will receive him. When he reached the top of the spiral staircase, he remained on the landing for a while, unsure about seizing the grotesque knocker that decorated the door to the studio in which Henri IV's painter, abandoned by Marie de Médicis in favor of Rubens, was no doubt working. The young man was experiencing that profound emotion that must have stirred the heart of all great artists when, at the height of their youth and love of art, they approached a man of genius or some masterpiece. There exists in all human feelings a pristine purity, engendered by a noble enthusiasm, that gradually grows weaker until happiness is only a memory, and glory a lie. Among these delicate emotions, the one most resembling love is the youthful ardor of an artist beginning the delicious torture of his destiny of glory and misfortune, an ardor full of audacity and shyness, of vague beliefs and inevitable discouragements. The man who, short of money but of budding genius, has never felt a sharp thrill when introducing himself to a

1

Honoré de Balzac

master, will always be lacking a string in his heart, some stroke of the brush, a certain feeling in his work, some poetic expressiveness. If a few braggarts, puffed up with themselves, believe in their future too soon, only fools consider them wise. Judging by this, the young stranger seemed to possess real merit, if talent can be measured by that initial shyness, by that indefinable modesty that men slated for glory are prone to lose during the practice of their art, just as pretty women lose theirs in the habits of coquetry. Being accustomed to triumph lessens one's self-doubt, and modesty may be a form of doubt.

Overwhelmed with poverty and, at that moment, surprised at his own presumptuousness, the poor novice wouldn't have entered the studio of the painter to whom we owe the admirable portrait of Henri IV if it hadn't been for an unusual helping hand sent his way by chance. An old man came up the stairs. From the oddness of his clothes, from the magnificence of his lace collar, from the exceptional self-assurance of his gait, the young man guessed that this person must be the painter's protector or friend; he moved back on the landing to give him room and studied him with curiosity, hoping to find in him the good nature of an artist or the helpful disposition of an art lover; but he discerned something diabolical in that face, and especially that indefinable something which attracts artists. Imagine a bald, convex, jutting forehead, sloping down to a small, flat nose turned up at the end like Rabelais' or Socrates'; a smiling, wrinkled mouth; a short chin, lifted proudly and adorned with a gray beard cut in a point; sea-green eyes apparently dimmed by age but which, through the contrast of the pearly white in which the irises swam, must sometimes cast hypnotic looks at the height of anger or enthusiasm. In addition, his face was singularly withered by the labors of old age, and still more by the kind of thoughts that hollow out both the soul and the body. His eyes had no more lashes, and only a few traces of eyebrows could be made out above their protruding ridges. Place this head on a thin, weak body, encircle it with sparkling-white lace of openwork like that of a fish slice, throw onto the old man's black doublet a heavy gold chain, and you will have an imperfect picture of that character, whom the feeble daylight of the staircase lent an additional tinge of the fantastic. You would have thought him a Rembrandt painting, walking silently without a frame in the dark atmosphere which that great painter made all his own. The old man cast a glance imbued with wisdom at the young man, knocked three times at the door, and said to the sickly man of about forty who opened it: "Good day, master."

Pourbus bowed respectfully; he let the young man in, thinking the old man had brought him along, and didn't trouble himself over him, especially since the novice was under the spell that born painters must undergo at the view of the first studio they've seen, where they can discover some of the practical methods of their art. A skylight in the vaulted ceiling illuminated Master Pourbus' studio. Falling directly onto a canvas attached to the easel, on which only three or four white lines had been placed, the daylight didn't reach the black depths of the corners of that vast room; but a few stray reflections in that russet shadow ignited a silvery flash on the belly of a knight's breastplate hung on the wall; streaked with a sudden furrow of light the carved, waxed cornice of an antique sideboard laden with curious platters; or jabbed with brilliant dots the grainy weave of some old curtains of gold brocade with large, sharp folds, thrown there as models. Plaster anatomical figures, fragments and torsos of ancient goddesses, lovingly polished by the kisses of the centuries, were strewn over the shelves and consoles. Innumerable sketches, studies in three colors of crayon, in sanguine, or in pen and ink, covered the walls up to the ceiling. Paintboxes, bottles of oil and turpentine, and overturned stools left only a narrow path to reach the aureole projected by the tall window, whose beams fell directly onto Pourbus' pale face and the peculiar man's ivory-colored cranium. The young man's attention was soon claimed exclusively by a painting which, in that time of chaos and revolutions, had already become famous and was visited by some of those obstinate men to whom we owe the preservation of the sacred fire in dark days. That beautiful canvas depicted Saint Mary of Egypt preparing to pay her boat fare.* That masterpiece, painted for Marie de Médicis, was sold by her when she had become destitute.

"I like your saint," the old man said to Pourbus, "and I'd pay ten gold *écus* for it over and above what the queen is paying; but, compete with her? Never!"

"You find it good?"

"Hm, hm!" said the old man. "Good? Yes and no. Your lady isn't badly set up, but she's not alive. You people think you've done it all when you've drawn a figure correctly and you've put everything in the right place according to the laws of anatomy! You color in that outline with a flesh tone prepared in advance on your palette, making sure to keep one side darker than the other, and because from time to time you look at a naked woman standing on a table, you think you've copied nature, you imagine you're painters and that you've stolen God's secrets! Brrr! To be a great poet, it's not enough to have a full command of

---

*This legendary figure was a prostitute before she converted to Christianity. Finding herself penniless on the way to Jerusalem, she offered a ship's captain her professional services in lieu of the fare.

syntax and avoid solecisms of language! Look at your saint, will you, Pourbus? At first glance she seems admirable; but at the second look, you notice that she's glued to the background and that you could never walk all around her. She's a silhouette with only one side, she's a cut-out likeness, an image that couldn't turn around or shift position. I feel no air between this arm and the field of the picture; space and depth are lacking; and yet the perspective is quite correct, and the atmospheric gradation of tones is precisely observed; but, despite such laudable efforts, I can't believe that that beautiful body is animated by the warm breath of life. It seems to me that, if I placed my hand on that bosom so firm and round, I'd find it as cold as marble! No, my friend, the blood isn't flowing beneath that ivory skin, life is not swelling with its crimson dew the veins and capillaries that intertwine in networks beneath the transparent amber of the temples and chest. This spot is throbbing, but this other spot is rigid; life and death are locked in combat in every detail: here she's a woman, there she's a statue, over there she's a corpse. Your creation is incomplete. You've been able to breathe only a portion of your soul into your beloved work. Prometheus' torch has gone out more than once in your hands, and many places in your painting haven't been touched by the heavenly flame."*

"But why is that, dear master?" Pourbus respectfully asked the old man, while the youngster had difficulty repressing a strong urge to strike him.

"Ah! This is it," said the little old man. "You've wavered indecisively between the two systems, between drawing and color, between the painstaking stolidity and precise stiffness of the old German masters and the dazzling fervor and felicitous richness of the Italian painters. You wanted to imitate Hans Holbein and Titian, Albrecht Dürer and Paolo Veronese, at the same time. Certainly that was a magnificent ambition! But what happened? You haven't achieved either the austere charm of dryness or the deceptive magic of chiaroscuro. In this spot here, like molten bronze cracking a mold that's too weak for it, Titian's rich, blonde color has smashed through the thin outline à la Dürer into which you had poured it. In other places, the outline resisted, and restrained the magnificent outpouring of the Venetian palette. Your figure is neither perfectly drawn nor perfectly painted, and everywhere it bears the traces of that unfortunate indecisiveness. If you didn't feel strong enough to weld together in the flame of your genius the two competing manners, you should have opted openly for one or the

---

*In Greek mythology, Prometheus created man and gave him fire, stolen from the gods.

other, so you could achieve that unity which simulates one of the conditions of life. You are true only in the interior sections; your outlines are false, they fail to join up properly, and they don't indicate that there's anything behind them. There's truth here," said the old man, pointing to the saint's chest. "And then here," he continued, indicating the place on the painting where the shoulder ended. "But here," he said, returning to the center of the bosom, "everything is false. Let's not analyze it, it would drive you to despair."

The old man sat down on a stool, held his head in his hands, and fell silent.

"Master," Pourbus said to him, "all the same, I studied that bosom from a nude live model; but, to our misfortune, there are true effects in nature that are no longer lifelike on the canvas . . ."

"The mission of art is not to copy nature but to express it! You're not a cheap copyist but a poet!" the old man exclaimed hotly, interrupting Pourbus with a lordly gesture. "Otherwise a sculptor would be through with all his labors if he just took a cast of a woman! Well now, just try taking a cast of your sweetheart's hand and setting it down in front of you; you'll find a hideous corpse that's not at all like the real thing, and you'll be compelled to seek out the chisel of a man who wouldn't copy it exactly for you, but would depict its movement and its life for you. Our job is to grasp the spirit, the soul, the face of objects and living beings. Effects! Effects! They're merely the incidental phenomena of life, not life itself. A hand, since I've chosen that example, a hand isn't merely part of a body, it expresses and prolongs an idea that must be grasped and rendered. Neither the painter, nor the poet, nor the sculptor should separate the effect from the cause, since they're inevitably interconnected! The real struggle is there! Many painters achieve an instinctive sort of success without knowing that theme of art. You draw a woman, but you don't see her! That's not the way to make nature yield up her secrets. Your hand, without any thought on your part, reproduces the model you had copied in your teacher's studio. You don't delve sufficiently into the intimate depths of the form, you don't pursue it with sufficient love and perseverance through its twists and turns and its elusive maneuvers. Beauty is something austere and difficult that cannot be attained that way; you have to wait for the right moment, spy it out, seize it, and hug it tight to force it to surrender. Form is a Proteus much more unseizable and rich in hidden secrets than the Proteus of legend;* it's only after lengthy struggles that you can compel it to show itself in its

---

*In Greek mythology, Proteus was a sea deity who rapidly changed into one shape after another in order to elude capture.

true guise; all of you are satisfied with the first semblance it yields to you, or at most the second, or the third; that's not how victorious fighters go about it! Those unvanquished painters don't allow themselves to be deceived by all those subterfuges; they persevere until nature is forced to show itself bare, in its true spirit. That's how Raphael went about it," said the old man, taking off his black velvet cap to show the respect he felt for the king of art; "his great superiority is due to the intimate sense which, in his works, seems set on breaking through form. In his figures, form is what it is in us, an interpreter of ideas and feelings, a great poetry. Every figure is a world, a portrait whose model appeared in a sublime vision, colored by light, pointed out by an inner voice, stripped bare by a heavenly finger that showed the sources of expression within the past of an entire lifetime. You make beautiful robes of flesh for your women, beautiful draperies of hair, but where is the blood that produces either calm or passion and causes particular effects? Your saint is a brunette, but this here, my poor Pourbus, is suitable for a blonde! And so your figures are pale, colored-in phantoms that you trot out before us, and you call that painting and art. Because you've produced something that looks more like a woman than like a house, you think you've hit the mark; and, really proud because you no longer need to label your figures *currus venustus* or *pulcher homo*,* the way the earliest painters did, you imagine you're wonderful artists! Ha, ha! You're not there yet, my worthy friends, you'll have to use up many a crayon and cover many a canvas before you get there. Of course, a woman carries her head this way, she holds her skirt like that, her eyes grow languid and melt with that air of resigned gentleness, that's the way that the fluttering shadow of her lashes hovers over her cheeks! It's right, and it isn't. What's missing? A trifle, but that trifle is everything. You have the semblance of life, but you aren't expressing its overflowing superabundance, that indefinable something, which may be the soul, hovering like a cloud above the outer husk; in short, that bloom of life which Titian and Raphael captured. Starting out from where you've left off, some excellent painting might be achieved; but you get tired too soon. The layman admires you, but the true connoisseur merely smiles. O Mabuse, my teacher," that odd character added, "you're a thief, you stole life when you died! — Aside from that," he resumed, "this canvas is better than the paintings of that brute Rubens, with his mountains of Flemish meat, sprinkled with vermilion, his tidal waves of red hair, and his glaring colors. At least you've got color, feeling, and drawing there, the three essential components of art."

---

*"Graceful chariot," "handsome man" (Latin).

"But that saint is sublime, my good man!" the young man called out loudly, emerging from his deep daydreams. "These two figures, the saint and the boatman, have a subtlety of purpose that the Italian painters have no notion of; I don't know one of them who could have created the indecisiveness of the boatman."

"Does this little rascal belong to you?" Pourbus asked the old man.

"Alas, master, forgive my boldness," replied the novice, blushing. "I'm a nobody, a dauber of pictures by instinct who has recently arrived in this city, which is the fount of all knowledge."

"Get to work!" Pourbus said to him, offering him a red crayon and a sheet of paper.

The stranger nimbly made a line copy of the Saint Mary.

"Oh, ho!" cried the old man. "Your name?"

The young man signed "Nicolas Poussin" at the bottom.

"That's not bad for a beginner," said the odd character who had been speaking so extravagantly. "I see that it's possible to talk about painting in your presence. I don't blame you for having admired Pourbus' saint. It's a masterpiece for the world at large, and only those initiated into the deepest secrets of art can discover what's wrong with it. But, since you're worthy of the lesson, and able to understand, I'm going to show you just how little it would take to complete this picture. Be all eyes and give me complete attention; another opportunity like this to teach you may never occur again. Your palette, Pourbus?"

Pourbus went to get a palette and brushes. The little old man rolled up his sleeves in a convulsively brusque fashion, stuck his thumb into the palette, mottled and laden with paints, that Pourbus held out to him; he not so much took as ripped from his hands a fistful of brushes of all sizes, and his pointy beard suddenly started bobbing in menacing motions that expressed the urgings of an ardent imagination. While loading his brush with paint, he muttered between his teeth: "Here are tints that are only good enough to be thrown out the window along with the man who mixed them; they're revoltingly crude and false, how can I paint with this?" Then, with feverish energy, he dipped the tip of his brush into the various gobs of paint, at times running through their entire gamut more rapidly than a cathedral organist races from one end of his keyboard to another during the Easter *O Filii*.

Pourbus and Poussin remained motionless on either side of the canvas, sunk in the most vehement contemplation.

"Do you see, young man," said the old man without turning away, "do you see how, with three or four strokes and a little bluish glaze, it was possible to make the air circulate around the head of this poor saint, who must have been stifled, trapped in that thick atmosphere? See how this drapery now flutters and how one now realizes that the breeze is lifting it! Before, it looked like a starched cloth held up by pins. Do you notice how the gleaming gloss I've just put on her chest reproduces the plump suppleness of a girl's skin, and how the tint blended of red-brown and burnt ocher warms up the gray chill of this large shadow, in which the blood was coagulating instead of flowing? Young man, young man, what I'm showing you here, no master could teach you. Mabuse alone possessed the secret of giving figures life. Mabuse had only one pupil: me. I never had any, and I'm old! You have enough intelligence to guess the rest from what I allow you to glimpse."

While speaking, the old man was placing strokes on every part of the painting: here two brushstrokes, there just one, but always so felicitously that you would have said it was a different picture, one bathed in light. He worked with such passionate fervor that beads of sweat stood out on his hairless brow; he moved so rapidly, with short movements that were so impatient and jerky, that it seemed to young Poussin as if the body of that peculiar character contained a demon acting through his hands, seizing them eerily as if against the man's will. The preternatural brightness of his eyes, the convulsions that looked like the effects of resistance, lent that notion a semblance of truth that had to affect a young imagination. The old man kept saying: "Bang, bang, bang! That's how it takes on consistency, young man! Come, little brushstrokes, make that icy tint grow red for me! Let's go!—Boom, boom, boom!" he would say, while adding warmth to the areas he had accused of lacking life, while eliminating the differences in feeling with a few patches of color, and restoring the unity of tone that an ardent Egyptian woman demanded.

"You see, youngster, it's only the final brushstroke that counts. Pourbus laid on a hundred and I've laid on just one. No one is going to thank us for what's underneath. Remember that!"

Finally that demon halted and, turning around to address Pourbus and Poussin, who were speechless with admiration, he said: "This is still not as good as my *Quarrelsome Beauty*, and yet it would be possible to put one's name at the bottom of a picture like this. Yes, I'd sign it," he added, standing up to fetch a mirror, in which he looked at it. "Now let's go dine," he said. "Both of you come to my house. I have smoked ham, I have good wine! Ho, ho! Despite the unfortunate era we live in, we'll chat about painting! We're equally matched. Here's a little fellow," he added, tapping Nicolas Poussin on the shoulder, "who has some aptitude."

Then, catching sight of the Norman's wretched coat, he drew a leather purse from his belt, rummaged in it, drew out two gold coins, and, showing them to him, said: "I'll buy your drawing."

"Take it," said Pourbus to Poussin, seeing him give a start and blush with shame, for that young adept had a poor man's pride. "Go on and take it; he's got enough in his moneybag to ransom two kings!"

The three of them left the studio and walked, conversing about the arts, until they reached a beautiful wooden house located near the Saint-Michel Bridge; its decorations, its door knocker, the frames of its casement windows, its arabesques, all amazed Poussin. The aspiring painter suddenly found himself in a low-ceilinged room, in front of a good fire, near a table laden with appetizing food, and, by unusual good fortune, in the company of two great artists who were exceptionally good-natured.

"Young man," Pourbus said to him, seeing him dumbfounded in front of a painting, "don't look at that picture too long, or it will drive you to despair."

It was the *Adam* that Mabuse painted to get out of the prison where his creditors kept him so long. Indeed, that figure gave such a strong impression of being real that, from that moment on, Nicolas Poussin began to understand the true meaning of the confused words the old man had uttered. The old man looked at the picture with seeming satisfaction, but without enthusiasm, and appeared to be saying: "I've done better!"

"There's life in it," he said. "My poor master outdid himself in it; but there was still a little truth missing in the background of the picture. The man is really alive; he's getting up and is going to approach us. But the air, sky, and wind that we breathe, see, and feel aren't there. Besides, he's still just a man! Now, the only man who ever came directly from the hands of God ought to have something divine about him, which is missing. Mabuse used to say so himself, with vexation, when he wasn't drunk."

Poussin was looking back and forth between the old man and Pourbus with restless curiosity. He came up to Pourbus as if to ask him their host's name; but the painter put a finger to his lips with an air of mystery, and the young man, though keenly interested, kept silent, hoping that sooner or later some remark would allow him to learn the name of his host, whose wealth and talents were sufficiently attested to by the respect Pourbus showed him and by the wonders assembled in that room.

Seeing a magnificent portrait of a woman on the somber oak paneling, Poussin exclaimed: "What a beautiful Giorgione!"

"No," replied the old man, "you're looking at one of my first smears."

"Damn! Then I'm in the home of the god of painting," Poussin said naïvely.

The old man smiled like a man long accustomed to such praise.

"Master Frenhofer," said Pourbus, "could you possibly send for a little of your good Rhenish wine for me?"

"Two casks," replied the old man. "One to repay you for the pleasure I had this morning looking at your pretty sinner, and the other as a present to a friend."

"Oh, if I weren't always under the weather," continued Pourbus, "and if you were willing to let me see your *Quarrelsome Beauty*, I could paint some tall, wide, deep picture in which the figures were life-size."

"Show my painting!" cried the old man, quite upset. "No, no, I still have to perfect it. Yesterday, toward evening," he said, "I thought I had finished it. Her eyes seemed moist to me, her flesh was stirring. The locks of her hair were waving. She was breathing! Even though I've found the way to achieve nature's relief and three-dimensionality on a flat canvas, this morning, when it got light, I realized my mistake. Oh, to achieve this glorious result, I've studied thoroughly the great masters of color, I've analyzed and penetrated layer by layer the paintings of Titian, that king of light; like that sovereign painter, I sketched in my figure in a light tint with a supple, heavily loaded brush—for shadow is merely an incidental phenomenon, remember that, youngster. Then I went back over my work and, by means of gradations and glazes that I made successively less transparent, I rendered the heaviest shadows and even the deepest blacks; for the shadows of ordinary painters are of a different nature from their bright tints; they're wood, bronze, or whatever you want, except flesh in shadow. You feel that, if their figure shifted position, the areas in shadow would never be cleared up and wouldn't become bright. I avoided that error, into which many of the most illustrious have fallen, and in my picture the whiteness can be discerned beneath the opacity of even the most dense shadow! Unlike that pack of ignoramuses who imagine they're drawing correctly because they produce a line carefully shorn of all rough edges, I haven't indicated the outer borders of my figure in a dry manner, bringing out even the slightest detail of the anatomy, because the human body isn't bounded by lines. In that area, sculptors can come nearer the truth than we can. Nature is comprised of a series of solid shapes that dovetail into one another. Strictly speaking, there's no such thing as drawing! Don't laugh, young man! As peculiar as that remark may sound to you, you'll understand the reasons behind it some day. Line is the means by which man renders the effect of light on objects; but there are no lines in nature, where everything is continuous: it's by modeling that we draw; that is, we separate things from the medium in which they exist; only the distribution of the light gives the body its appearance! Thus, I haven't fixed any outlines, I've spread over the contours a cloud of blonde, warm intermediate tints in such a way that no one can put his finger on the exact place where the contours meet the background. From close up, this work looks fleecy and seems lacking in precision, but, at two paces, everything firms up, becomes fixed, and stands out; the body turns, the forms project, and you feel the air circulating all around them. And yet I'm still not satisfied, I have some doubts. Perhaps it's wrong to draw a single line, perhaps it would be better to attack a figure from the center, first concentrating on the projecting areas that catch most of the light, and only then moving on to the darker sections. Isn't that how the sun operates, that divine painter of the universe? O nature, nature, who has ever captured you in your inmost recesses? You see, just like ignorance, an excess of knowledge leads to a negation. I have doubts about my painting!"

The old man paused, then resumed: "It's ten years now, young man, that I've been working on it; but what are ten short years when it's a question of struggling with nature? We don't know how long it took Sir Pygmalion to make the only statue that ever walked!"

The old man dropped into deep musing, and sat there with fixed eyes, mechanically playing with his knife.

"Now he's in converse with his 'spirit,'" said Pourbus quietly.

At that word, Nicholas Poussin felt himself under the power of an unexplainable artistic curiosity. That old man with white eyes, attentive and in a stupor, had become more than a man to him; he seemed like a fantastic genius living in an unknown sphere. He awakened a thousand confused ideas in his soul. The moral phenomenon of that type of fascination can no more be defined than one can render in words the emotion caused by a song that reminds an exiled man's heart of his homeland. The scorn this old man affected to express for beautiful artistic endeavors, his wealth, his ways, Pourbus' deference toward him, that painting kept a secret for so long—a labor of patience, a labor of genius, no doubt, if one were to judge by the head of the Virgin that young Poussin had so candidly admired, and which, still beautiful even alongside Mabuse's *Adam*, bespoke the imperial talents of one of the princes of art—everything about that old man exceeded the boundaries of human nature. The clear, perceivable image that Nicolas Poussin's rich imagination derived from his observation of that preternatural being was a total image of the artistic nature, that irrational nature to which such great powers have been entrusted, and which all too often abuses those powers, leading cool reason, the bourgeois, and even some connoisseurs over a thousand rocky roads where there is nothing for them, while that white-winged lass, a madcap of fantasies, discovers there epics, castles, works of art. Nature—mocking and kind, fertile and poor! And so, for the enthusiastic Poussin, that old man, through a sudden transfiguration, had become art itself, art with its secrets, its passions, and its daydreams.

"Yes, my dear Pourbus," Frenhofer resumed, "up to now I've been unable to find a flawless woman, a body whose contours are perfectly beautiful, and whose complexion . . . But," he said, interrupting himself, "where is she in the living flesh, that undiscoverable Venus of the ancients, so often sought for, and of whose beauty we scarcely come across even a few scattered elements here and there? Oh, if I could see for a moment, just once, that divine, complete nature—in short, that ideal—I'd give my entire fortune; but I'd go after you in the underworld, heavenly beauty! Like Orpheus, I'd descend to the Hades of art to bring back life from there."

"We can leave," said Pourbus to Poussin; "he can't hear us any more or see us any more!"

"Let's go to his studio," replied the amazed young man.

"Oh, the sly old customer has taken care to block all entry to it. His treasures are too well guarded for us to reach them. I didn't wait for your suggestion or your fancies to attempt an attack on the mystery."

"So there is a mystery?"

"Yes," Pourbus replied. "Old Frenhofer is the only pupil Mabuse was ever willing to train. Having become his friend, his rescuer, his father, Frenhofer sacrificed the largest part of his treasures in satisfying Mabuse's passions; in exchange, Mabuse transmitted to him the secret of three-dimensionality, the power to give figures that extraordinary life, that natural bloom, which is our eternal despair, but the technique of which he possessed so firmly that, one day, having sold for drink the flowered damask with which he was supposed to make garments to wear at Emperor Charles V's visit to the city, he accompanied his patron wearing paper clothing painted like damask. The particular brilliance of the material worn by Mabuse surprised the emperor, who, wanting to compliment the old drunkard's protector on it, discovered the deception. Frenhofer is a man who's impassioned over our art, who sees higher and further than other painters. He has meditated profoundly on color, on the absolute truth of line; but, by dint of so much investigation, he has come to have doubts about the very thing he was investigating. In his moments of despair, he claims that there is no such thing as drawing and that only geometric figures can be rendered in line; that is going beyond the truth, because with line and with black, which isn't a color, we can create a figure; which proves that our art, like nature, is made up of infinite elements: drawing supplies a skeleton, color supplies life; but life without the skeleton is even more incomplete than the skeleton without life. Lastly, there's something truer than all this: practice and observation are everything to a painter, and if reasoning and poetry pick a fight with our brushes, we wind up doubting like this fellow here, who is as much a lunatic as he is a painter. Although a sublime painter, he had the misfortune of being born into wealth, and that allowed his mind to wander. Don't imitate him! Work! Painters shouldn't meditate unless they have their brushes in their hand."

"We'll make our way in!" cried Poussin, no longer listening to Pourbus and no longer troubled by doubts.

Pourbus smiled at the young stranger's enthusiasm, and left him, inviting him to come and see him.

Nicolas Poussin went back slowly toward the Rue de la Harpe, walking past the modest hostelry in which he lodged, without noticing it. Climbing his wretched straicase with restless speed, he reached a high-ceilinged room located beneath a half-timbered roof, that naïve, light-weight covering of old Parisian houses. Near the dark window, the only one in his room, he saw a girl, who, at the sound of the door, suddenly stood up straight, prompted by her love; she had recognized the painter by the way he had jiggled the latch.

"What's the matter?" she asked.

"The matter, the matter," he cried, choking with pleasure, "is that I really felt I was a painter! I had doubted myself up to now, but this morning I began to believe in myself! I can be a great man! Come, Gillette, we'll be rich and happy! There's gold in these brushes."

But he suddenly fell silent. His serious, energetic face lost its expression of joy when he compared the immensity of his hopes to the insignificance of his resources. The walls were covered with plain pieces of paper full of crayon sketches. He didn't own four clean canvases. Paints were expensive at the time, and the poor gentleman's palette was nearly bare. Living in such destitution, he possessed and was aware of incredible riches of the heart and the superabundance of a devouring genius. Brought to Paris by a nobleman who had befriended him, or perhaps by his own talent, he had suddenly found a sweetheart there, one of those noble, generous souls who accept suffering at the side of a great man, adopting his poverty and trying to understand his whims; brave in poverty and love just as other women are fearless in supporting luxury and making a public show of their lack of feelings. The smile that played on Gillette's lips gilded that garret, competing with the brightness of the sky. The sun didn't always shine, whereas she was always there, communing with her passion, devoted to her happiness and her suffering, consoling the genius that overflowed with love before taking possession of art.

"Listen, Gillette, come."

The joyful, obedient girl leaped onto the painter's knees. She was all grace, all beauty, lovely as springtime, adorned with all feminine riches and illumining them with the flame of a beautiful soul.

"Oh, God!" he cried. "I'll never have the courage to tell her."

"A secret?" she asked. "I want to hear it."

Poussin remained quiet, lost in thought.

"Well, talk."

"Gillette, my poor sweetheart!"

"Oh, you want something from me?"

"Yes."

"If you want me to pose for you again the way I did the other day," she continued in a rather sulky way, "I'll never agree to it again, because, at times like that, your eyes no longer tell me anything. You no longer think about me, even though you're looking at me."

"Would you prefer to see me drawing another woman?"

"Maybe," she said, "if she were good and ugly."

"So, then," Poussin went on in a serious tone, "what if, for my future glory, in order to make me a great painter, it were necessary to pose for someone else?"

"You want to test me," she said. "You know very well I wouldn't go."

Poussin's head dropped onto his chest, like that of a man succumbing to a joy or sorrow too strong for his soul.

"Listen," she said, tugging the sleeve of Poussin's threadbare doublet, "I've told you, Nick, that I'd give my life for you; but I've never promised you to give up my love for you while I was alive."

"Give it up?" cried Poussin.

"If I showed myself that way to somebody else, you wouldn't love me anymore. And I myself would feel unworthy of you. Isn't catering to your whims a natural, simple thing? In spite of myself, I'm happy, and even proud to do everything you ask me to. But for somebody else—oh, no."

"Forgive me, Gillette," said the painter, falling on his knees. "I'd rather be loved than famous. For me you're more beautiful than wealth and honors. Go, throw away my brushes, burn those sketches. I was wrong. My calling is to love you. I'm not a painter, I'm a lover. Art and all its secrets can go hang!"

She admired him, she was happy, delighted! She ruled supreme, she felt instinctively that the arts were forgotten for her sake and cast at her feet like a grain of incense.

"And yet he's only an old man," Poussin continued. "He'll only be able to see the woman in you. You're so perfect!"

"I've got to love you!" she cried, prepared to sacrifice her romantic scruples to reward her lover for all the sacrifices he made for her. "But," she went on, "it would mean ruining me. Ah, to ruin myself for you!

Yes, it's a beautiful thing, but you'll forget me. Oh, what a terrible idea you've come up with!"

"I've come up with it, and I love you," he said with a kind of contrition, "but it makes me a scoundrel."

"Shall we consult Father Hardouin?" she asked.

"Oh, no. Let it be a secret between the two of us."

"All right, I'll go; but you mustn't be there," she said. "Remain outside the door, armed with your dagger; if I scream, come in and kill the painter."

No longer seeing anything but his art, Poussin crushed Gillette in his arms.

"He doesn't love me any more!" Gillette thought when she was alone.

She already regretted her decision. But she soon fell prey to a fear that was even crueler than her regret; she did her best to drive away an awful thought that was taking shape in her heart. She was thinking that she already loved the painter less, suspecting him of being less estimable than before.

2. Catherine Lescault

Three months after Poussin and Pourbus first met, Pourbus paid a visit to Master Frenhofer. The old man was at the time a prey to one of those spontaneous fits of deep discouragement, the cause of which, if one is to believe the firm opinions of traditional doctors, is indigestion, the wind, heat, or some bloating of the hypochondriac regions; but, according to psychologists, is really the imperfection of our moral nature. The man was suffering from fatigue, pure and simple, after trying to finish his mysterious painting. He was seated languidly in an enormous chair of carved oak trimmed with black leather; and, without abandoning his melancholy attitude, he darted at Pourbus the glance of a man who had settled firmly into his distress.

"Well, master," Pourbus said, "was the ultramarine you went to Bruges for bad? Weren't you able to grind your new white? Is your oil defective, or your brushes stiff?"

"Alas!" exclaimed the old man, "for a moment I thought my picture was finished; but now I'm sure I was wrong about a few details, and I won't be calm until I've dispelled my doubts. I've decided to take a trip to Turkey, Greece, and Asia to look for a model and compare my picture to different types of natural beauties. Maybe," he went on, with a smile of satisfaction, "I've got nature herself upstairs. Sometimes I'm

almost afraid that a breath of air might wake up that woman and she
might disappear."

Then he suddenly rose, as if to depart.

"Oh, oh," Pourbus replied, "I've come just in time to save you the ex-
pense and fatigue of the journey."

"How so?" asked Frenhofer in surprise.

"Young Poussin has a sweetheart whose incomparable beauty is totally flawless. But, dear master, if he agrees to lend her to you, at the
very least you'll have to show us your canvas."

The old man just stood there, motionless, in a state of complete
stupefaction.

"What!" he finally cried in sorrow. "Show my creation, my wife?
Rend the veil with which I've chastely covered my happiness? But that
would be a terrible prostitution! For ten years now I've been living with
this woman; she's mine, only mine, she loves me. Hasn't she smiled at
me at each brushstroke I've given her? She has a soul, the soul that I
endowed her with. She would blush if anyone's eyes but mine were
fixed on her. Show her! But where is the husband or lover so vile as to
lead his wife to dishonor? When you paint a picture for the royal court,
you don't put your whole soul into it; all you're selling to the courtiers
is colored dummies. My kind of painting isn't painting, it's emotion,
passion! She was born in my studio, she must remain there as a virgin,
she can only leave when fully dressed. Poetry and women only surrender themselves naked to their lovers! Do we possess Raphael's model,
Ariosto's Angelica, Dante's Beatrice? No, we only see their forms! Well,
the picture I have under lock and key upstairs is something exceptional
in our art. It isn't a canvas, it's a woman!—a woman with whom I weep,
laugh, converse, and think. Do you want me suddenly to throw away
ten years' happiness the way one throws off a coat? Do you want me
suddenly to leave off being a father, a lover, God? That woman isn't a
single creature, she's all of creation. Let your young man come; I'll give
him my treasures, I'll give him pictures by Correggio, Michelangelo,
Titian; I'll kiss the print of his feet in the dust; but make him my rival?
Shame upon me! Ha, ha, I'm even more of a lover than I am a painter.
Yes, I'll have the strength to burn my *Quarrelsome Beauty* with my
dying breath; but to expose her to the eyes of a man, a young man, a
painter? No, no! If anyone sullied her with a glance, I'd kill him the
next day! I'd kill you on the spot, you, my friend, if you didn't salute her
on your knees! Now do you want me to submit my idol to the cold eyes
and stupid criticisms of imbeciles? Oh, love is a mystery, it lives only in
the depths of our heart, and everything is ruined when a man says, even
to his friend, 'This is the woman I love!'"

The old man seemed to have become young again; his eyes shone and were full of life; his pale cheeks were mottled with a vivid red, and his hands were trembling. Pourbus, astonished at the passionate vehemence with which those words were uttered, had nothing to say in reply to a sentiment that was as novel as it was profound. Was Frenhofer in his right mind or mad? Was he under the spell of some artistic fancy, or were the ideas he had expressed the result of that indescribable fanaticism produced in us by the long gestation of a great work? Could one ever hope to come to terms with that odd passion?

A prey to all these thoughts, Pourbus said to the old man: "But isn't it one woman for another? Isn't Poussin exposing his sweetheart to your eyes?"

"Some sweetheart!" Frenhofer replied. "She'll betray him sooner or later. Mine will always be faithful to me!"

"All right," Pourbus continued, "let's drop the subject. But before you find, even in Asia, a woman as beautiful and perfect as the one I'm talking about, you may die without finishing your picture."

"Oh, it's finished," said Frenhofer. "Anyone who looked at it would imagine he saw a woman lying on a velvet bed beneath curtains. Near her, a golden tripod emits incense. You'd be tempted to take hold of the tassel of the cords that hold back the curtains, and you'd think you saw the bosom of Catherine Lescault, a beautiful courtesan nicknamed the Quarrelsome Beauty, heaving with her breath. And yet, I'd like to be sure . . ."

"Well, go to Asia," Pourbus replied, detecting a sort of hesitation in Frenhofer's eyes.

And Pourbus took a few steps toward the door of the room.

At that moment, Gillette and Nicolas Poussin had arrived near Frenhofer's dwelling. As the girl was about to go in, she freed herself from the painter's arm and recoiled as if gripped by some sudden presentiment.

"But what am I coming here for?" she asked her lover in deep tones, staring at him.

"Gillette, I've left it all up to you, and I want to obey you in all ways. You are my conscience and my glory. Come back home; I'll be happier, maybe, than if you . . ."

"Am I my own mistress when you speak to me that way? Oh, no, I'm only a child.—Let's go," she added, seeming to make a violent effort; "if our love dies and I'm laying in long days of regret for myself, won't your fame be the reward for my obedience to your wishes? Let's go in; being a kind of eternal memory on your palette will be like being still alive."

On opening the door to the house, the two lovers came upon Pourbus; amazed at the beauty of Gillette, whose eyes were full of tears

at the moment, he took hold of her as she stood there trembling and, leading her in to the old man, said:
"Now, isn't she worth all the masterpieces in the world?"
Frenhofer gave a start. There was Gillette, in the naïve, simple attitude of an innocent, frightened girl of Caucasian Georgia who has been kidnapped and is being presented by brigands to a slave dealer. A modest blush gave color to her face, she lowered her eyes, her hands hung at her sides, her strength seemed to desert her, and tears protested against the violence being done to her modesty. At that moment, Poussin, in despair at having let that beautiful treasure out of his garret, cursed himself. He became a lover foremost and an artist next; a thousand scruples tortured his heart when he saw the rejuvenated eyes of the old man, who, as painters do, was mentally undressing the girl, divining her most secret forms. Then he reverted to the fierce jealousy of true love.
"Gillette, let's go!" he cried.
At that tone, at that cry, his joyful sweetheart raised her eyes in his direction, saw him, and rushed into his arms.
"Oh, you do love me!" she replied, bursting into tears.
After having had the energy to be silent about her suffering, she had no more strength left to conceal her happiness.
"Oh, leave her with me for just a while," said the old painter, "and you'll compare her to my Catherine. Yes, I consent."
There was still love in Frenhofer's cry. He seemed to have a lover's vanity for his painted woman and to be enjoying in advance the victory that his virgin's beauty would win over that of a real girl.
"Don't let him go back on his word!" cried Pourbus, tapping Poussin on the shoulder. "The fruits of love are quickly gone, those of art are immortal."
Looking hard at Poussin and Pourbus, Gillette replied, "Am I nothing more than a woman to him?" She raised her head proudly; but when, after darting a fierce glance at Frenhofer, she saw her lover busy contemplating once again the portrait he had recently taken for a Giorgione, she said:
"Ah! Let's go upstairs! He's never looked at me that way."
"Old man," Poussin resumed, torn from his meditation by Gillette's voice, "do you see this sword? I'll thrust it into your heart at the first word of complaint this girl utters; I'll set fire to your house, and no one will get out alive. Understand?"
Nicolas Poussin was somber, and his words were awesome. This attitude, and especially the young painter's gesture, consoled Gillette, who almost forgave him for sacrificing her to the art of painting and his glorious future. Pourbus and Poussin remained at the studio door, looking

at each other in silence. If at first the painter of St. *Mary of Egypt* permitted himself a few exclamations—"Ah, she's getting undressed, he's asking her to stand in the daylight! He's comparing her!"—soon he fell silent at the sight of Poussin, whose face showed deep sadness. And, even though elderly painters no longer feel such petty scruples in the presence of art, he admired them for being so naïve and charming. The young man kept his hand on his sword guard and his ear almost glued to the door. The two of them, standing there in the darkness, thus looked like two conspirators awaiting the moment when they would strike down a tyrant.

"Come in, come in," called the old man, beaming with happiness. "My picture is perfect, and now I can show it with pride. Never will a painter, brushes, paints, canvas, or light create any rival to Catherine Lescault, the beautiful courtesan."

Prey to a keen curiosity, Pourbus and Poussin rushed into the midst of a vast studio covered with dust, in which everything was in disorder, in which they saw here and there pictures hung on the walls. They first stopped in front of a life-size woman's figure, half draped, for which they were overcome with admiration.

"Oh, don't bother about that," said Frenhofer, "it's a canvas I daubed over to study a pose, it's a worthless picture. Here are my mistakes," he went on, showing them captivating compositions hanging on the walls all around them.

At these words, Pourbus and Poussin, dumbfounded at this contempt for works of that merit, looked for the portrait they had been told about, but failed to catch sight of it.

"Well, here it is!" said the old man, whose hair was mussed, whose face was inflamed with a preternatural excitement, whose eyes sparkled, and who was panting like a young man drunk with love. "Ah, ha!" he cried. "You weren't expecting so much perfection! You're standing in front of a woman, and looking for a picture. There's such great depth to this canvas, the air in it is so real, that you can no longer distinguish it from the air that surrounds us. Where is art? Lost, vanished! Here are the very forms of a girl. Haven't I really captured her coloring, the lifelikeness of the line that seems to bound her body? Isn't it the same phenomenon that's offered to us by objects that exist within the atmosphere just as fish live in water? Don't you admire the way the contours stand out from the background? Don't you imagine that you could run your hand down that back? Thus, for seven years, I studied the effects of the mating of daylight and objects. And that hair, doesn't the light inundate it? . . . But she drew a breath, I think! . . . That bosom, see? Oh, who wouldn't want to worship her on his knees? The flesh is throbbing. She's going to stand up, just wait."

"Can you make out anything?" Poussin asked Pourbus.

"No. What about you?"

"Not a thing."

The two painters left the old man to his ecstasy, and looked to see whether the light, falling vertically onto the canvas he was showing them, wasn't neutralizing all its effects. Then they examined the painting, placing themselves to the right, to the left, straight in front of it, stooping down and getting up again in turns.

"Yes, yes, it's really a canvas," Frenhofer said to them, misunderstanding the purpose of that careful scrutiny. "Look, here's the stretcher, the easel; finally, here are my paints, my brushes."

And he took hold of a brush that he showed them in a naïve gesture.

"The sly old fox is having a joke with us," said Poussin, coming back in front of the so-called painting. All I see there is colors in a jumbled heap, contained within a multitude of peculiar lines that form a wall of paint."

"We're wrong. See?" Pourbus said.

Coming closer, they could discern in a corner of the canvas the tip of a bare foot emerging from that chaos of colors, tints, and vague nuances, a sort of shapeless mist; but a delicious foot, a living foot! They stood awestruck with admiration before that fragment which had escaped from an unbelievable, slow and progressive destruction. That foot appeared there like the torso of some Parian marble Venus rising up out of the ruins of a city that had been burned to the ground.

"There's a woman underneath all this!" cried Pourbus, indicating to Poussin the layers of paint that the old painter had set down on over the other, in the belief that he was making his painting perfect.

The two painters spontaneously turned toward Frenhofer, beginning to understand, though only vaguely, the state of ecstasy in which he existed.

"He's speaking in good faith," said Pourbus.

"Yes, my friend," replied the old man, awakening, "one must have faith, faith in art, and one must live with one's work for a long time in order to produce a creation like this. Some of these shadows cost me many labors. Look, on the cheek, beneath the eyes, there's a light penumbra that, if you observe it in nature, will seem all but uncapturable to you. Well, do you think that that effect didn't cost me unheard-of pains to reproduce? But also, dear Pourbus, look at my piece attentively and you'll understand more fully what I was telling you about the way to handle modeling and contours. Look at the light on the bosom and see how, by a series of strokes and highlights done in heavy impasto, I succeeded in catching true daylight and combining it with the gleaming whiteness of the illuminated areas; and how, to achieve the converse effect, eliminating the ridges and grain of the paint, I was able, by dint of caressing the figure's contour, which is submerged in demitints, to remove the very notion of a drawn line and such artificial procedures, and to give it the very look and solidity of nature. Come close, you'll see better how I worked. From a distance, it can't be seen. There! In this spot, I think, it's highly remarkable."

And with the tip of his brush he pointed out a blob of bright paint to the two artists.

Pourbus tapped the old man on the shoulder, turning toward Poussin. "Do you know that we have a very great painter in him?" he said.

"He's even more of a poet than a painter," Poussin replied gravely.

"This," continued Pourbus, touching the canvas, "is the extreme limit of our art on earth."

"And from there it gets lost in the skies," said Poussin.

"How many pleasures in this bit of canvas!" exclaimed Pourbus.

The old man, absorbed, wasn't listening to them but was smiling at that imaginary woman.

"But sooner or later he'll notice that there's nothing on his canvas!" cried Poussin.

"Nothing on my canvas!" said Frenhofer, looking by turns at the two painters and at his so-called picture.

"What have you done?" Pourbus replied to Poussin.

The old man gripped the young man's arm violently, saying: "You see nothing, vagabond, good-for-nothing, cad, catamite!* Why did you come up here, anyway?—My dear Pourbus," he went on, turning to that painter, "could you too be making fun of me? Answer me! I'm your friend; tell me, have I really spoiled my picture?"

Pourbus, undecided, didn't dare say a thing; but the anxiety depicted on the old man's pallid face was so cruel that he pointed to the canvas and said: "Just look!"

Frenhofer studied his picture for a moment and tottered.

"Nothing, nothing! And after working ten years on it!"

He sat down and began weeping.

"So I'm just an imbecile, a lunatic! So I have no talent, no ability; I'm just a rich man who, when he walks, merely walks! So I haven't created anything!"

He studied his canvas through his tears. Suddenly he stood up with pride, and darted a furious glance at the two painters.

"By the blood, body, and head of Christ, you are envious men trying

---

*The insults are somewhat archaic, indicating that Frenhofer has regressed to the sixteenth century.

to make me believe that she's ruined, so you can steal her from me! *I can see her!*" he cried. "She's wonderfully beautiful."

At that moment, Poussin heard the weeping of Gillette, who had been forgotten in a corner.

"What's wrong, angel?" the painter asked her, suddenly becoming a lover again.

"Kill me!" she said. "I'd be a low creature if I still loved you, because I have contempt for you. I admire you, and you horrify me. I love you, and I think I hate you already."

While Poussin was listening to Gillette, Frenhofer was covering up his Catherine with a green serge, as gravely calm as a jeweler locking up his drawers because he thinks that skillful thieves are present. He threw the two painters a profoundly crafty look, full of scorn and suspicion, and silently turned them out of his studio, with convulsive haste. Then, on the threshold of his home, he said to them: "Farewell, my little friends."

That leavetaking chilled the heart of the two painters. The next day, Pourbus, worried, came to see Frenhofer again, and was informed that he had died during the night after burning his canvases.

AN EPISODE DURING THE TERROR

TO MONSIEUR GUYONNET-MERVILLE: I think it's only right, my dear former employer, to explain to those who are curious about everything where I was able to learn enough about legal matters to conduct the business of my little world; and only right to honor here the memory of the affable and witty man who, meeting Scribe, another amateur clerk, at a ball, said to him: "Why not stop by my office? I'm sure some work can be found for you." But do you need this public testimony to be certain of the author's affection?

On January 22, 1793, about eight in the evening, in Paris, an old lady was walking down the steep rise that comes to an end in front of the church of Saint-Laurent in the Faubourg Saint-Martin. It had snowed so much during the day that footsteps could hardly be heard. The streets were deserted. The altogether natural fear the silence inspired was heightened by all the terror under which France was then groaning; thus, the old lady had not yet met up with anybody; moreover, her sight, weak for some time now, didn't allow her to make out in the distance, by the light of the streetlamps, a few thinly scattered passersby, like shadows in the immense thoroughfare of that faubourg. She was walking alone courageously across that solitude, as if her age were a charm bound to protect her from any misfortune.

After passing by the Rue des Morts, she thought she could discern the heavy, firm step of a man walking behind her. It occurred to her that this wasn't the first time she had heard that sound; she took fear at having been followed, and tried to walk even more swiftly in order to reach a shop that was quite brightly lit, hoping she could verify in the light the suspicions that had gripped her. As soon as she was within the horizontal beam of light issuing from that shop, she turned her head sharply and half made out a human form in the fog; that indistinct sight was enough for her, she staggered a moment beneath the weight of the terror that overwhelmed her, for by then she no longer doubted that she had been escorted by the unknown man from the very first step she had taken outside of her residence, and the desire to escape from a spy

23

lent her strength. Incapable of thinking things out, she doubled her
pace, as if she could elude a man who was surely more agile than she
was. After running for a few minutes, she arrived at a pastry shop, went
in, and fell rather than sat down on a chair placed in front of the cash
desk. At the moment she made the door latch squeak, a young woman
busy with embroidery raised her eyes and, through the panes of the
shop window, recognized the old-fashioned violet silk mantle in which
the old lady was wrapped, and hastened to open a drawer as if to take
from it something she needed to hand to her. Not only did the motions
and features of the young woman express the desire to get rid of the
stranger quickly, as if she were the kind of person one isn't happy to see,
but she also manifested an expression of impatience when she found
the drawer empty; then, without looking at the lady, she dashed out of
the cashier's box, headed for the back room, and called her husband,
who appeared at once.

"Well, where did you put . . .?" she asked him with an air of mystery,
indicating the old lady with a look and not finishing her sentence.

Although the pastryman could only see the enormous black silk bon-
net, circled with knots of violet ribbon, that constituted the stranger's
headgear, he vanished after throwing his wife a glance that seemed to
say "Do you think I'm going to leave that in your cash desk?"

Surprised at the old lady's silence and motionlessness, the shop-
keeper's wife approached her again; and, looking at her, she felt gripped
by a strong feeling of pity or perhaps also curiosity. Although the woman's
complexion was naturally sallow, like that of a person devoted to secret
austerities, it was easy to discern that a recent emotion made her extraor-
dinarily pale. Her hat was arranged so as to hide her hair, which was no
doubt white with age; for the clean condition of her dress collar showed
that she wore no powder. This lack of ornament made her face acquire
a sort of religious severity. Her features were serious and proud. In the
past the manners and habits of the people of quality were so different
from those of people belonging to other classes that it was easy to recog-
nize one of the nobility. Thus the young woman was convinced that the
stranger was a former aristocrat and had belonged to the royal court.

"Madame? . . ." she said to her involuntarily and respectfully, forgetting that such a term of address was forbidden.*

The old lady didn't reply. She kept her eyes glued to the shop window, as if some terrifying thing had been drawn on it.

"What's wrong, citizen?" asked the proprietor, who reappeared
immediately.

---

*After the Revolution, the terms *monsieur* and *madame* were considered to be a relic of
the old aristocracy and were replaced by the egalitarian *citoyen* and *citoyenne*.

The citizen pastryman brought the lady out of her musing as he handed her a little cardboard box wrapped in blue paper.

"Nothing, nothing, friends," she answered in a soft voice.

She lifted her eyes toward the pastryman as if to throw him a look of thanks; but, seeing a red cap* on his head, she uttered a cry.

"Oh! You've betrayed me? . . ."

The young woman and her husband replied with a shocked gesture that made the stranger blush, either because she had suspected them or because she was pleased.

"Excuse me," she then said with childlike sweetness. Then, taking a gold *louis* from her pocket, she presented it to the pastryman. "This is the price we agreed on," she added.

There is a poverty that the poor can guess at. The pastryman and his wife looked at each other and indicated the old woman to each other, sharing a single thought. That gold *louis* must be her last. The lady's hands were trembling as she held out that coin, which she looked at with sorrow but without greed; yet she seemed aware of the full extent of her sacrifice. Fasting and indigence were engraved on her face in lines as clear as those of fear and ascetic habits. Her clothes showed traces of former splendor. They were of worn-out silk; a clean, if faded, mantle; carefully mended lace; in short, opulence in tatters! The shopkeepers, torn between pity and self-interest, began by soothing their conscience with words.

"But, citizen, you seem quite weak."

"Would Madame need to eat something?" the wife continued, interrupting her husband.

"We have some very good bouillon," said the pastryman.

"It's so cold out, Madame may have become chilled walking; but you can rest here and warm up a little."

"We aren't as bad as we're painted!" exclaimed the pastryman.

Won over by the benevolent tone that enlivened the words of the charitable shopkeepers, the lady confessed that she had been followed by a man, and that she was afraid to return home alone.

"Is that all?" replied the man in the red cap. "Wait for me, citizen."

He gave the *louis* to his wife. Then, stirred by the kind of gratitude that slips into a merchant's soul when he receives an exorbitant price for a commodity of moderate value, he went to put on his National Guard† uniform, took his hat, girded on his short sword, and reappeared in arms; but his wife had had time to reflect. As in many

---

*Official headgear for members of the commune of Paris, also worn by dedicated citizens of the new republic.
†The citizens' militia formed at the outset of the Revolution.

another heart, reflection closed the open hand of benevolence. Worried, afraid to find her husband mixed up in some bad business, the pastryman's wife tried to pull the tail of his coat to hold him back; but, in obedience to a feeling of charity, the good man immediately offered himself to the old lady as an escort.

"It seems that the man the citizen is afraid of is still prowling in front of the shop," the young woman said excitedly.

"I'm afraid so," the lady said naïvely.

"What if he's a spy? What if it's a conspiracy? Don't go out there, and take back the box from her . . ."

Those words, whispered in the pastryman's ear by his wife, froze the impromptu courage that had possessed him.

"Oh, I'm going out to tell him a thing or two, and get rid of him for you right away," exclaimed the pastryman, opening the door and dashing out.

The old lady, passive as a child and nearly numb, sat back down on her chair. Before very long, the honest merchant reappeared; his face, quite florid by nature and further reddened by the fire of his oven, had suddenly become pale; he was shaken by such a great fright that his legs were trembling and his eyes looked like those of a drunken man.

"Do you want to make us lose our heads, filthy aristocrat?" he shouted in a rage. "Show us your heels, never turn up here again, and don't count on me to supply you with material for a conspiracy!"

Finishing this speech, the pastryman tried to take back from the old lady the box she had put in one of her pockets. Hardly had the pastryman's bold hands touched her clothes when the stranger, preferring to chance the dangers of the road with no defender but God, rather than losing what she had just bought, recovered the agility of her youth; she darted toward the door, opened it briskly, and vanished from the sight of the stupefied, trembling husband and wife.

As soon as the stranger was outside, she started walking rapidly; but her strength soon failed her, for she heard the spy by whom she was relentlessly followed, making the snow creak beneath his heavy steps; she was compelled to stop, and he stopped; she didn't dare speak to him or look at him, either because of the fear that gripped her or because she didn't have her wits about her. She continued along her way, walking slowly; then the man slackened his pace so as to remain at a distance that allowed him to keep his eye on her. The strange man seemed like that old woman's own shadow. The bells were ringing nine when the silent pair once more passed in front of the church of Saint-Laurent. It lies in the nature of every soul, even the feeblest, that a feeling of calm follows a violent agitation, because there may be no end to emotions but our mental capacity is limited. Thus, the unknown woman, having experienced no harm from her imagined persecutor, decided to take him for a secret friend eager to protect her; she put together all the circumstances that had attended the appearances of the stranger as if to find plausible motives for that comforting view, and it then pleased her to discover that his intentions were good rather than bad. Forgetting the fright the man had just given the pastryman, she therefore walked on with firm strides through the upper reaches of the Faubourg Saint-Martin. After a half hour's walk, she arrived at a house situated near the fork formed by the main street of the faubourg and the street that leads to the Pantin tollgate. This spot is still one of the most deserted anywhere in Paris. The wintry wind, passing over the hills of Saint-Chaumont and Belleville, was whistling through the houses, or rather huts, widely scattered in this almost uninhabited valley, in which the properties are divided by walls made of earth and bones. This desolate location seemed to be the natural refuge of poverty and despair. The man who was doggedly pursuing the poor creature bold enough to cross those silent streets at night seemed awestruck at the spectacle that met his eyes. He remained pensive, standing in an attitude of hesitation, under the feeble light of a streetlamp whose vague gleam barely pierced the fog. Fear lent eyes to the old lady, who thought she saw something sinister in the stranger's features; she felt her terrors reawakening, and took advantage of the seeming uncertainty that held the man back by slipping into the darkness in the direction of the doorway of the solitary house; she worked a spring and vanished with supernatural speed. The man, motionless, observed that house, which in a way was representative of the wretched dwellings of that neighborhood. This tumbledown shanty built of rubble was covered with a coat of yellowing plaster so heavily cracked that you were afraid it would collapse at the slightest puff of wind. The roof, made of brown tiles and covered with moss, was sagging in several places so you'd think it would give way beneath the weight of the snow. Each story had three windows, whose frames, rotted by humidity and disjointed by the effects of sunlight, indicated that the cold surely must penetrate into the rooms. This isolated house resembled an old tower that time still forgot to destroy. A feeble light illumined the casement windows that irregularly punctuated the garret which crowned this poor edifice; while the rest of the house was in total darkness.

It was an effort for the old woman to climb the rough, coarse staircase, along which a rope took the place of a railing to lean upon; she knocked furtively at the door of the dwelling that was located in the garret, and hastily sat down on a chair that an old man offered her.

"Hide, hide!" she said to him. "Even though we go out so very seldom, our activities are known, our journeys are spied on."

"What new has happened?" asked another old woman seated near the fire.

"The man who's been prowling around the house since yesterday followed me this evening."

At those words, the three inhabitants of that hovel looked at one another, their faces showing the signs of extreme terror. The old man was the least upset of the three, perhaps because he was in the greatest danger. Under the weight of a great misfortune or under the yoke of persecution, a brave man begins to sacrifice himself, as it were, he considers each new day merely as one more victory over fate. The eyes of the two women, glued on that old man, promptly revealed that he was the sole object of their intense concern.

"Why lose hope in God, Sisters?" he said in a muffled but fervidly pious voice. "We once sang His praises amid the cries uttered by the murderers and the dying at the Carmelite convent.* If He decided to rescue me from that slaughter, it was no doubt to save me for a destiny that I must accept without complaining. God protects His own, He can dispose of them as He sees fit. It's you, not me, that we should be worrying about."

"No," said one of the two old women, "what does our life count for compared with a priest's?"

"Once I found myself outside the abbey of Chelles, I looked upon myself as dead!" exclaimed the nun who hadn't gone out.

"Here," said the one who had just arrived, "here are the wafers. But," she cried, "I hear someone climbing the stairs!"

At those words, all three started to listen. The sound stopped.

"Don't be frightened," said the priest, "if someone tries to make his way to where you are. A person whose fidelity we can count on is sure to have taken every step necessary for crossing the border, and will come to pick up the letters I've written to the Duc de Langeais and the Marquis de Beauséant, so that they can devise a way to snatch you out of this horrible country, out of the death or destitution that awaits you here."

"Then, you won't come along?" the two nuns gently cried, with a measure of despair.

"My place is wherever there are victims," the priest said matter-of-factly.

They fell silent and looked at their guest in holy admiration.

"Sister Marthe," he said, addressing the nun who had gone out for

---

*This may refer to the famous arrest and guillotining of Carmelite nuns by revolutionaries, an incident that has inspired songs, stories, and the opera by Francis Poulenc, *Dialogues of the Carmelites*.

the wafers; "this messenger is to reply '*Fiat voluntas*'* to the watchword '*Hosanna.*'"

"There's someone on the stairs!" cried the other nun, opening a hiding place that had been installed in the roof.

This time, amid the deepest silence, it was easy to hear a man's steps resounding on the stair treads, which were covered with hard lumps of dried mud. The priest squeezed painfully into a sort of closet, and the nun threw some old clothes over him.

"You can close it, Sister Agathe," he said in a stifled voice.

Hardly had the priest hidden when three knocks on the door made the two holy women start; they looked at each other questioningly without uttering a word. Each of them seemed to be about sixty. Separated from the world for forty years, they were like plants accustomed to the atmosphere of a hothouse, plants that die if you remove them from it. Used to convent life, they were unable to conceive of any other. One morning, their grilles having been broken, they had trembled to find themselves free. It's easy to imagine the sort of induced weakness of mind that the events of the Revolution had created in their innocent souls. Unable to adjust their conventual notions to the difficulties of life, and not even understanding their situation, they were like children who had been taken care of up till then and who, deprived of their mother's protection, now prayed instead of clamoring. Thus, in the face of the danger they foresaw at that moment, they remained mute and passive, knowing no defense other than Christian resignation. The man seeking admission interpreted that silence in his own way; he opened the door and revealed himself all of a sudden. The two nuns trembled when they recognized the person who, for some time, had been prowling around their house and making inquiries about them; they remained motionless, observing him with a nervous curiosity, like wild children who examine strangers in silence. This man was tall and heavy; but nothing in his actions, appearance, or face indicated a bad man. He imitated the nuns' immobility, slowly casting glances all around the room he stood in.

Two straw mats placed on boards served as a bed for the two nuns. A single table stood in the center of the room, and on it were a copper candlestick, a few plates, three knives, and a round loaf of bread. The blaze in the fireplace was low. A few sticks of wood piled up in a corner were further testimony to the poverty of the two recluses. The walls, covered with a coat of very old paint, attested to the bad condition of the roofing, for stains resembling brown nets showed where rainwater had seeped in. A relic, no doubt rescued from the sack of the abbey of

---

*"Thy will be done."

Chelles, adorned the fireplace mantelpiece. Three chairs, two chests, and a poor commode completed the furnishings of the room. A door located near the fireplace led one to conjecture that there was a second room.

The inventory of the cell was quickly taken by the man who had entered within that household under such frightening auspices. A feeling of pity was reflected on his face, and he cast a benevolent glance at the two women; he was at least as embarrassed as they were. The strange silence in which all three remained was soon broken, for the stranger, finally guessing the moral weakness and inexperience of the two poor creatures, said to them in a voice he strove to make gentle: "I haven't come here as an enemy, citizens." He stopped, then resumed, saying: "Sisters, if you should meet with some misfortune, please believe that I had nothing to do with it. I have a favor to ask of you . . ."

They still kept silent.

"If I'm disturbing you, if . . . I'm inconveniencing you, please speak freely . . . I'll leave; but I must tell you that I'm completely at your service; that, if there's anything I can do for you, you can make use of me without fear; and that I alone, perhaps, am above the law, since there is no more king . . ."

There was such a tone of truth in his words that Sister Agathe, the one of the two nuns who belonged to the Langeais family, and whose manners seemed to indicate that she had once known the splendor of festivities and had breathed the air of the court, hastened to point to one of the chairs, as if asking their guest to be seated. The stranger showed a kind of joy mingled with sadness as he understood her gesture, but didn't take a seat until the two respectable maidens had sat down.

"You have given refuge," he resumed, "to a venerable nonjuring priest* who miraculously escaped the Carmelite massacres."

"*Hosanna!*" said Sister Agathe, interrupting the stranger and looking at him with an uneasy curiosity.

"I don't believe that's his name," he replied.

"But, sir," Sister Marthe said hastily, "we have no priest here, and. . ."

"In that case, you should have more care and foresight," the stranger replied softly, stretching out his arm toward the table and picking up a breviary. "I don't think you know Latin, and . . ."

He didn't continue, for the extraordinary emotion depicted on the faces of the two poor nuns made him fear he had gone too far; they were trembling, and their eyes filled with tears.

---

*A priest who refused to subscribe to the 1790 Civil Constitution of the Clergy, which in effect severed the French church from the Vatican.

"Be reassured," he said to them in a candid voice, "I know your guest's name and yours, and for three days now I've known about your distress and your devotion to the venerable Abbé de . . ."

"Sh!" said Sister Agathe naïvely, putting a finger to her lips.

"You see, Sisters, that, if I had formed the horrible purpose of betraying you, I could already have accomplished it more than once . . ."

Hearing those words, the priest squeezed out of his prison and reappeared in the center of the room.

"I'm unable to believe, sir," he said to the stranger, "that you are one of our persecutors, and I put my trust in you. What do you want of me?"

The holy confidence shown by the priest, the nobility diffused through all his features, would have disarmed murderers. The mysterious person who had come and injected life into that scene of poverty and resignation observed for a moment the group formed by those three beings; then, assuming a confidential tone, he addressed the priest in these terms: "Father, I've come to beg you to celebrate a funeral mass for the repose of the soul . . . of a . . . of a sacred person whose body will never rest in hallowed ground . . ."

The priest shuddered involuntarily. The two nuns, not yet understanding who the stranger was talking about, kept straining their necks and turning their faces toward the two interlocutors, in an attitude of curiosity. The ecclesiastic studied the stranger: an unmistakable anxiety was reflected on his face, and his eyes were expressive of ardent supplications.

"All right," replied the priest, "come back tonight at midnight, and I'll be ready to celebrate the only funeral service we can offer in expiation of the crime of which you speak . . ."

The stranger gave a start, but a satisfaction, sweet and serious at the same time, appeared to win out over a secret sorrow. After respectfully taking leave of the priest and the two holy maidens, he vanished, manifesting a sort of mute gratitude that was understood by those three noble souls. About two hours after that scene, the stranger returned, knocked discreetly at the garret door, and was shown in by Mademoiselle de Beauséant, who led him into the second room of that poor hovel, where every preparation had been made for the ceremony. Between two chimney flues, the two nuns had brought in the old commode whose old-fashioned outlines were hidden beneath a magnificent altar cloth of green watered silk. A large ebony and ivory crucifix, hanging on the yellow wall, made its bareness more obvious and drew all eyes powerfully toward itself. Four small, thin tapers, which the sisters had managed to keep upright on that improvised altar by holding them down with sealing wax, cast a pale gleam, only fitfully reflected on the wall. That feeble light barely illumined the rest of the room; but,

by lending its glow solely to the sacred objects, it was like a ray falling
from heaven upon that unadorned altar. The tile floor was damp. The
roof, which sloped down steeply on both sides, as in attics, had several
cracks through which a glacial wind blew in. Nothing was less splen-
did, and yet nothing, perhaps, was more solemn than that gloomy ceremony. A deep silence, which would have allowed them to hear the
quietest call of a person passing along the Route d'Allemagne, cast a
sort of somber majesty over that nocturnal scene. In short, the grandeur
of the action contrasted so sharply with the poverty of the surroundings
that a feeling of religious awe was generated. On either side of the altar,
the two old recluses, kneeling on the floor tiles with no concern for
their deadly dampness, were praying along with the priest, who, wearing his ecclesiastical robes, was arranging a gold chalice adorned with
precious stones, a sacred vessel rescued, no doubt, from the sack of the
abbey of Chelles. Next to this vessel, a magnificent gift from a king, the
water and wine prepared for the holy sacrifice were contained in two
glasses that were hardly worthy of the lowest tavern. Having no missal,
the priest had placed his breviary on a corner of the altar. An ordinary
plate was on hand for washing those innocent hands, guiltless of blood-
shed. Everything was gigantic but small, poor but noble, profane and
holy at the same time.

The stranger came and knelt down piously between the two nuns.
But suddenly, noticing black crepe on the chalice and the crucifix (for,
having nothing with which to signalize the intent of this funeral mass,
the priest had dressed God himself in mourning), he was overcome by
such a powerful recollection that beads of sweat stood out on his broad
forehead. Thereupon the four silent actors of that scene looked at one
another mysteriously; then their souls, influencing one another emu-
lously, communicated their feelings to one another in that way and
were mingled in religious pity: it was as if their minds had recalled the
martyr whose remains had been consumed by quicklime; as if his
shade stood there before them in all its royal majesty. They celebrated
a funeral mass without the body of the deceased. Beneath those disjointed roof tiles and slats, four Christians were about to intercede with
God for a king of France and perform his last rites without a coffin. It
was the purest of all devotions, an astonishing act of fidelity accomplished with no ulterior motives. Surely in the eyes of God it was like
the charitable glass of water that weighs as much in the balance as the
greatest virtues. The entire monarchy was there, in the prayers of a
priest and two poor maidens; but perhaps the revolution was also
represented by that man whose face betrayed so much remorse that
anyone had to believe he was fulfilling the vows of an enormous
repentance.

Instead of pronouncing the Latin words *"Introibo ad altare Dei,"* etc.,* the priest, by divine inspiration, looked at the other three present, who stood for Christian France, and said to them in French, in order to counter the indigence of that hovel: "We shall enter into the sanctuary of God!"

At those words, pronounced with deepest fervor, a holy dread gripped the listening man and the two nuns. Even beneath the vaults of Saint Peter's in Rome, God would not have shown himself in greater majesty than He did then to the eyes of those Christians in that poverty-stricken refuge: so true is it that, between Him and man, no intermediary seems necessary, and that He derives His grandeur from Himself alone. The stranger's fervor was genuine. Thus the emotion that united the prayers of those four servants of God and king was unanimous. The holy words resounded like heavenly music amid the silence. There was one moment when tears got the better of the stranger, at the *Pater noster*. The priest added to it this Latin prayer, which was surely understood by the stranger: *Et remitte scelus regicidis sicut Ludovicus eis remisit semetipse* (And forgive the regicides just as Louis XVI himself forgave them).

The two nuns saw two heavy tears trace a moist path down the stranger's virile cheeks and fall onto the floor. The office of the dead was recited. The *Domine salvum fac regem*,† chanted in a low voice, sadly affected these loyal monarchists, who recalled that the child king, for whom they were beseeching the Almighty at that moment, was a captive in the hands of his enemies. The stranger shuddered at the thought that a new crime could be committed in which he would surely be compelled to participate. When the funeral service was over, the priest made a sign to the two nuns, who withdrew. As soon as he was alone with the stranger, he walked over to him with a gentle, sad air, then said to him in a paternal voice: "My son, if you have dipped your hands in the blood of the martyred king, trust in me. There is no fault that, in the eyes of God, cannot be erased by a repentance as touching and sincere as yours appears to be."

At the first words spoken by the ecclesiastic, the stranger, in spite of himself, gave an indication of terror; but he resumed a calm bearing and looked at the astonished priest with self-assurance: "Father," he said, in a noticeably shaky voice, "no one is more innocent than I of the blood that has been shed . . ."

"I must believe you," said the priest . . .

He paused while studying his penitent once again; then, persisting

---

*"I shall enter and approach the altar of God."
†"God save the king."

in taking him for one of those timorous members of the Convention who handed over an inviolable, hallowed head in order to save their own, he continued in a grave voice: "My son, remember that, to be absolved of this great crime, it is not sufficient not to have had a direct hand in it. Those who were able to defend the king but left their swords in their sheath, will have a very heavy account to settle before the King of Heaven . . . Oh, yes," added the old priest, shaking his head from right to left with an expressive motion, "yes, very heavy! . . . because, by remaining inactive, they became the involuntary accomplices of that frightful crime . . ."

"Do you believe," asked the dumbfounded stranger, "that an indirect participation will be punished? . . . Is the soldier guilty who was assigned to stand in line at the occasion?"

The priest was undecided. Happy over the dilemma in which he was placing that Puritan of royalty—between the dogma of passive obedience, which, according to the partisans of the monarchy, ought to prevail in military regulations, and the equally major dogma that consecrates the respect due to the person of kings—the stranger eagerly saw in the priest's hesitation a favorable solution of doubts that seemed to torment him. Then, so as not to let the venerable Jansenist reflect any longer, he said: "I'd be ashamed to offer you any fee for the funeral service you have just celebrated for the repose of the king's soul and for soothing my conscience. An inestimable action can only be repaid by an offering that is itself priceless. Therefore, sir, deign to accept the gift I make you of a holy relic . . . A day may perhaps come when you will understand its value."

Saying these words, the stranger presented to the ecclesiastic a small, extremely lightweight box; the priest took it almost involuntarily, for the solemnity of that man's words, the tone in which he spoke, the respect with which he had held that box, had caused him tremendous surprise. Then they returned to the room in which the two nuns were awaiting them.

"You are," the stranger said to them, "in a house whose owner, Mucius Scaevola, the plasterer who lives on the second floor, is famous in the neighborhood for his patriotism; but in secret he is an adherent of the Bourbons. He was formerly a groom of the Prince de Conti and owes his fortune to him. If you don't leave his house, you'll be safer here than anywhere else in France. Stay here. Pious persons will see to your needs, and you can await better times without danger. In a year, on January twenty-first,"—in uttering these last words, he couldn't repress an involuntary start—"if you adopt this miserable spot as a refuge, I will return and celebrate the expiatory mass with you . . ."

He broke off. He greeted the mute inhabitants of the garret, cast a final glance at the material tokens of their destitution, and vanished.

For the two innocent nuns, an adventure like that one was as interesting as a storybook; thus, as soon as the venerable abbé had informed them of the mysterious present so solemnly offered by that man, they placed the box on the table, and the three worried figures, feebly lit by the tallow candle, betrayed an indescribable curiosity. Mademoiselle de Langeais opened the box and found in it a very fine cambric handkerchief, soiled with sweat; unfolding it, they discovered stains.

"It's blood!" said the priest.

"It's marked with the royal crown!" exclaimed the other sister.

The two sisters dropped the precious relic in their horror. For those two naïve souls, the mystery enveloping the stranger became inexplicable; and, as for the priest, from that day on he didn't even attempt to seek an explanation.

Before long the three prisoners, despite the Terror, noticed that a powerful hand was extended over them. First, they received firewood and provisions; then, the two nuns guessed that a woman was associated with their protector, when they were sent linens and clothes that would allow them to go out without calling attention to the aristocratic style of the garments they had been compelled to keep; finally, Mucius Scaevola gave them two citizen's identification cards. Frequently, information necessary to the priest's safety came to him in roundabout ways; and he observed that this advice arrived at such opportune moments that it had to come from a person privy to state secrets. Despite the famine oppressing Paris, the outlaws found at the door of their hovel rations of *white bread* regularly left there by invisible hands; nevertheless, they thought they could identify Mucius Scaevola as the mysterious agent of that charity, which was as ingenious as it was intelligent. The noble inhabitants of the garret had no doubt but that their protector was the person who had come to celebrate the expiatory mass on the night of January 22, 1793; thus, he became the object of a very special devotion for those three beings, who hoped in him alone and lived through him alone. They had added special prayers for him to their regular prayers; morning and evening, those pious souls made wishes for his happiness, prosperity, and welfare; they begged God to keep him safe from every ambush, to deliver him from his enemies, and to grant him a long, peaceful life. Their gratitude, which was renewed daily, so to speak, was of necessity combined with a feeling of curiosity that became livelier from day to day. The circumstances that had attended the stranger's appearance was the subject of their conversations, they made countless conjectures about him, and the distraction he supplied them with was another benefaction of a new type. They promised one another not to let the stranger go without expressing their friendship on the evening he came back, as he had promised, to celebrate the sad anniversary of the death of Louis XVI. That night, so impatiently awaited, finally arrived. At midnight, the sound of the stranger's heavy steps was heard on the old wooden staircase; the room had been decorated to receive him, the altar was prepared. This time, the sisters opened the door in advance, and both of them hastened to light the stairs. Mademoiselle de Langeais even walked down a few steps to catch sight of her benefactor sooner.

"Come," she said to him in an emotional, loving voice, "come . . . you've been expected."

The man raised his head, cast a somber glance at the nun, but didn't reply; she felt as if a garment of ice had fallen upon her, and kept silent; at the sight of him, gratitude and curiosity were extinguished in all their hearts. He was perhaps less cold, less taciturn, less terrifying, than he appeared to those souls, whose exalted spirits disposed them toward a warm display of friendship. The three poor prisoners, who understood that that man wished to remain a stranger to them, resigned themselves. The priest thought he noticed on the man's lips a smile, quickly repressed, when he caught sight of the preparations that had been made for entertaining him; he heard the mass and prayed; but he vanished after declining with a few polite words the invitation extended by Mademoiselle de Langeais to share in the little collation they had prepared.

After the Ninth of Thermidor, the nuns and the Abbé de Marolles were able to walk about in Paris without running the slightest risk. On his first walk outside, the old priest went to a perfume shop, at the sign of the Queen of Flowers, run by the citizens Ragon, former purveyors of perfume to the court who had remained loyal to the royal family, and whom the Vendéens* made use of to correspond with the princes and the royalist committee in Paris. The abbé, dressed in the fashions of the time, was on the doorstep of that shop, located between the church of Saint-Roch and the Rue des Frondeurs, when a crowd that filled the Rue Saint-Honoré prevented him from leaving.

"What's going on?" he asked Madame Ragon.

"It's nothing," she replied, "it's the tumbril and hangman heading for the Place Louis XV. Oh, we saw it often last year; but today, four days after the anniversary of January twenty-first, it's possible to see that awful procession without any grief."

"Why?" asked the abbé. "What you're saying is unchristian."

"Oh, it's the execution of Robespierre's accomplices; they defended

_____
*Counterrevolutionaries in the west of France.

themselves as much as they were able to; but it's their turn now to go where they sent so many innocent people."

A crowd that filled the Rue Saint-Honoré passed by like an ocean wave. Above their heads, the Abbé de Marolles, yielding to an impulse of curiosity, saw standing on the tumbril the man who three days earlier had been listening to his mass . . .

"Who is that?" he asked, "the man who . . ."

"He's the hangman," replied Monsieur Ragon, using the old royal-era term for the public executioner.

"Husband, husband!" cried Madame Ragon, "the Abbé is dying."

And the old lady fetched a flask of vinegar to bring around the old priest, who had fainted.

"I'm sure now," he said, "that he gave me the handkerchief with which the king mopped his brow on the way to his martyrdom . . . Poor man! . . . The steel blade had a heart when all of France was without one! . . ."

The perfumers thought the poor priest was delirious.

FACINO CANE

I WAS LIVING at the time on a little street you surely don't know, the Rue de Lesdiguières: it begins at the Rue Saint-Antoine, opposite a fountain near the Place de la Bastille, and ends at the Rue de La Cerisaie.

The love of learning had cast me into a garret, where I worked at night, spending the daytime in a nearby library, that of Monsieur. I lived frugally, having accepted all the conditions of the monastic life, so essential to hard workers.

When the weather was good, I might walk for a while on the Boulevard Bourdon. One passion alone drew me away from my studious habits—but wasn't that also study of a kind? I went out to observe the customs of the neighborhood, its inhabitants and their character. Dressed as poorly as the laborers, caring nothing about decorum, I didn't put them on their guard against me; I could mingle in their groups and watch them making their deals and arguing when they finished their work for the day.

My powers of observation had already become intuitive, penetrating the soul while not disregarding the body; or, rather, they grasped the outer details so firmly that they immediately passed beyond them; they gave me the ability to live the life of the individual on which they focused, allowing me to take his place, just as the dervish in the *Arabian Nights* took on the body and soul of the people over whom he uttered certain words.

When, between eleven and midnight, I would come across a laborer and his wife returning together from the Ambigu-Comique Theater, I would amuse myself by following them from the Boulevard du Pont-aux-Choux to the Boulevard Beaumarchais. Those worthy people would first speak about the play they had seen; little by little they would get down to their own concerns; the mother would tug her child by the hand, paying no attention to its laments or requests; the married couple would count the money they would be paid the next day, planning to spend it in twenty different ways.

Then came details about the household, complaints about the exorbitant price of potatoes, or how long the winter was lasting and how the cost of peat fuel was going up; forceful protestations about how much they owed the baker; finally, arguments that became nasty, in which each of them would reveal his character in picturesque phrases.

Listening to these people, I was able to see myself in their place; I felt their rags on my back, I walked with my feet in their torn shoes; their desires, their needs were all transferred into my soul, or my soul was transferred into theirs. It was a waking dream. I would get angry along with them at the workshop foremen who tyrannized them, or at the bad customers who made them come back time after time without paying them.

To doff one's own habits, to become someone else through an intoxication of the moral faculties, and to play that game at will, such was my diversion. To what do I owe this gift? Is it second sight? Is it one of those capacities the abuse of which would lead to madness? I've never investigated the causes of this power; I possess it and I use it, and that's that. Let me merely say that, beginning with that period, I had decomposed the elements of that heterogeneous mass called the common folk, that I had analyzed it in such a way as to be able to evaluate its good or bad qualities.

I already knew how useful that neighborhood could be—that hotbed of revolutions containing heroes, inventors, applied scientists, rogues, scoundrels, virtues and vices, all oppressed by poverty, stifled by need; drowned in wine, worn out by strong liquor.

You can't imagine all the lost adventures, all the forgotten dramas in that city of sorrow! So many horrible and beautiful things! Imagination will never conceive the reality hidden there, and no one can discover it; one must descend too low to find those admirable scenes, either tragic or comic, masterpieces engendered by chance.

I don't know how I have kept to myself, without divulging it, the story I'm about to tell you; it's one of those curious narratives left in the sack from which memory draws them capriciously like numbers in a lottery: I have many others, just as unusual as this one and just as deeply buried; but they'll have their turn, believe me.

One day my charwoman, the wife of a laborer, came and asked me to honor with my presence the wedding of one of her sisters. To help you understand what sort of wedding that could be, I must inform you that I paid forty sous a month to that poor creature, who came every morning to make my bed, clean my shoes, brush my clothes, sweep the room, and prepare my lunch. The rest of the day she would go and turn the crank of some machine, earning ten sous a day at that hard trade. Her husband, a cabinetmaker, earned four francs. But, as that household included three children, they could scarcely eat a decent meal.

I've never come across honesty as solid as that man's and that woman's.

After I left that quarter, for five years Mother Vaillant came to congratulate me on my nameday, bringing me a bouquet and oranges, she who never had ten sous saved up. Poverty had made us close. I was never able to give her more than ten francs, often borrowed for the occasion. This may explain my promise to attend the wedding; I expected to take refuge in the joy of those poor people.

The party, the dance, all took place at a wineseller's on the Rue de Charenton, one floor up, in a large room lit by lamps with tinplate reflectors, papered with a greasy paper up to table height, and furnished with wooden benches along its walls. In that room eighty people in their Sunday best, adorned with bouquets and ribbons, all animated by the spirit of the Courtille,* their faces flushed, were dancing as if the world were coming to an end. The newlyweds kissed to everyone's satisfaction, and there were facetious ho-ho's and ha-ha's that were actually less indecent than the shy but meaningful glances of well-brought-up girls. Everyone here was expressing an animal contentment that had something contagious about it.

But neither the facial characteristics of that gathering, nor the wedding, nor anything about those people is connected with my story. Merely keep in mind the oddness of the setting. Imagine the cheap locale, painted red, smell the wine, listen to those howls of joy; remember you're in that neighborhood, in the midst of those laborers, those old men, those poor women given over to the pleasure of a single night!

The orchestra was made up of three blind men from the hospice of the Quinze-Vingts; the first played the violin, the second the clarinet, and the third the flageolet. The three were paid a total of seven francs for the night. At that price they naturally weren't offering Rossini or Beethoven, but playing what they felt like and what was within their ability; nobody blamed them for that—what charming tact! Their music assailed the eardrums so brutally that, after casting a glance at the gathering, I looked at that trio of blind men, and became disposed to be indulgent as soon as I recognized their uniform.

Those performers were sitting in the recess of a casement window; to make out their features, therefore, one had to get close to them. I didn't go over at once but, when I did come near, I can't say why, that

---

*The Courtille was an area in northeastern Paris known since the Middle Ages for its rowdy taverns and dance halls as well as for its elaborate masquerade processions during Carnival.

settled the matter; the wedding and its music vanished, and my curiosity was aroused to its highest pitch, for my soul was transferred into the body of the clarinet player. Both the violinist and the flageolet player had common faces, the well-known blind man's face, full of strain, attentive and serious; but that of the clarinetist was one of those phenomena that bring the artist and the philosopher to a sudden halt.

Picture the plaster death mask of Dante illuminated by the red gleam of the oil lamps and topped by a thicket of silvery white hair. The bitter, sorrowful expression of that magnificent head was heightened by his blindness, for the dead eyes were brought back to life by strength of thought; a sort of burning glow emanated from them, produced by a single, incessant desire energetically engraved on a convex brow crossed by wrinkles that were like the courses of an old stone wall.

This old man was blowing his instrument at random, without paying the least attention to the beat or the tune; his fingers descended or ascended, shaking the old keys out of mechanical routine; he wasn't embarrassed over producing what in orchestral terms are called "sour notes"; the dancers didn't notice them any more than my Italian's two acolytes did; you see, I wanted him to be an Italian, and he *was* an Italian.

Something grand and despotic was to be found in this old Homer who kept within himself an *Odyssey* doomed to oblivion. It was a grandeur so real that it even triumphed over his abject state, it was a despotism so vivid that it overcame his poverty.

None of the violent passions that lead a man to goodness or evil, that make him a convict or a hero, was lacking in that face, nobly chiseled, of an Italian olive hue, shaded by graying eyebrows that cast their shadow onto deep cavities, in which you feared to see the light of thought reappear, just as people are afraid to see a group of brigands, armed with torches and daggers, appear at the mouth of a cave.

A lion was pent up in that cage of flesh, a lion whose fury had been exhausted in vain against the iron of his bars. The blaze of despair had fallen to ashes and gone out, the lava had cooled; but the furrows, the upheavals, and a little smoke bore witness to the violence of the eruption, the ravages of the fire.

These ideas, awakened by this man's looks, were as hot in my soul as they were cold on his face.

After every quadrille, the violinist and the flageolet player, seriously occupied with their glass and their bottle, hung their instruments from the button of their reddish frock coats, and stretched out their hands toward a little table, placed in the recess of the casement, where their own private bar was located, and, each time, they offered the Italian a full glass, which he couldn't reach on his own because the table was behind his chair; each time, the clarinetist thanked them with a friendly nod of his head. Their movements were carried out with that precision which is always a surprising trait of the Quinze-Vingts blind, and which almost makes you think they can see. I approached the three blind men to listen to them; but, when I was near them, they studied me, no doubt realized I couldn't be one of the laborers, and kept silent.

"Where are you from, clarinet player?"

"From Venice," replied the blind man, with a slight Italian accent.

"Were you born blind, or did you become blind through . . ."

"Through an accident," he replied sharply, "from a damned gutta serena."*

"Venice is a beautiful city; I've always dreamed about going there."

The old man's features lit up, his wrinkles stirred, he felt a violent emotion.

"If I went there with you, you wouldn't waste your time," he said to me.

"Don't talk to him about Venice," the violinist said to me, "or you'll get our Doge going again; not to mention that he's already got two bottlefuls in his belly, the prince!"

"Come on, let's go, old man Canard,"† said the flageolet player.

All three started playing; but during the time it took them to play the four quadrilles, the Venetian was smelling me out, guessing the enormous interest I had in him. His face dropped its cold expression of sadness; a hope of some kind brightened every feature and spread among his wrinkles like a blue flame; he smiled and wiped his brow, that bold and awesome brow; finally he became merry, like a man climbing onto his hobbyhorse.

"How old are you?" I asked him.

"Eighty-two!"

"How long have you been blind?"

"For almost fifty years now," he replied, in a tone that indicated that his regrets were not merely for his loss of sight but also for some great power of which he had been deprived.

"Why do they call you the Doge?" I asked him.

"Oh, as a joke," he said to me. "I'm a patrician of Venice, and I could have become Doge as readily as anyone else."

"What's your name, then?"

---

*Gutta serena, or amaurosis, is a deterioration of the optic nerve, causing blindness but not leaving any other outward visible signs of its presence.

†A pun, using the French word *canard*, which in some contexts means "sour note," instead of the man's name.

"Here," he said, "I'm old man Canet. They've never been able to write my name any other way in their records. But in Italian, I'm Marco Facino Cane, Prince of Varese."

"What? You're descended from that notorious condottiere Facino Cane whose conquests were turned over to the dukes of Milan?"

"È vero,"* he said. "At that time, in order not to be killed by the Visconti, Cane's son took refuge in Venice and had himself inscribed in the Golden Book.† But now neither the Canes nor the book exist any more." And he made a frightening gesture, denoting a patriotism that had been snuffed out and a disgust for human affairs.

"But if you were a senator of Venice, you ought to be rich; how did you happen to lose your fortune?"

At that question, he raised his head toward me, as if to contemplate me in a really tragic upwelling of emotion, and replied: "In the misfortunes!"

He gave no more thought to drinking; with a gesture he declined the glass of wine the old flageolet player held out to him at that moment, then he lowered his head. These details were not such as to lessen my curiosity. During the quadrille those three automata played, I contemplated the old Venetian nobleman with the emotions that devour a twenty-year-old. I saw Venice and the Adriatic, I saw them in ruins on that ruined face. I was strolling in that city so beloved by its inhabitants, I went from the Rialto to the Grand Canal, from the Riva degli Schiavoni to the Lido; I returned to the cathedral, sublime in so original a manner; I looked at the windows of the Ca' d'Oro, each of which has a different decoration; I contemplated those old palaces so rich with marble; in short, all those wonders with which the scholar is all the more in sympathy when he paints them according to his fancy and doesn't drain the poetry from his dreams by viewing the reality.

I was tracing back the events in the life of this scion of the greatest of condottieri, seeking the imprints of his misfortunes and the causes of that deep physical and moral degradation that made even more beautiful the sparks of grandeur and nobility that had been revivified at that moment. Our thoughts were certainly shared, for I believe that blindness makes mental communication much more rapid by preventing one's attention from being dispersed among external objects. The proof of our meeting of minds was not long in coming.

Facino Cane stopped playing, stood up, came over to me, and addressed me with a "Let's get out of here!" that affected me like an electric shock. I gave him my arm, and we left.

---

*"It's true," in Italian.
†Venetian registry of the nobility.

When we were out on the street, he said to me:

"Are you willing to take me to Venice, to lead me there? Are you willing to trust me? You'll be richer than the ten richest firms in Amsterdam or London, richer than the Rothschilds—in short, as rich as the *Arabian Nights*."

I thought the man was crazy; but in his voice was a power I obeyed. I let myself be led, and he took me over to the moat of the Bastille as if he could see. He sat down on a stone in a very solitary spot where later on they built the bridge linking the Canal Saint-Martin with the Seine. I took a seat on another stone in front of that old man, whose white hair was shining like silver threads in the moonlight. The silence, scarcely broken by the rumbling that reached us from the boulevards, the purity of the night, everything helped make that scene truly fantastic.

"You talk to a youngster about millions, and you think he'd hesitate to endure a thousand ills to obtain them! Aren't you pulling my leg?"

"May I die without confession," he said to me truculently, "if what I'm going to tell you isn't true.

"I was twenty years old just as you are now, I was rich, I was good-looking, I was a nobleman. I started my career with the greatest of all follies, love. I loved in a way people no longer love, to the point of climbing into a chest and risking being killed by a dagger there, and all without receiving anything but the promise of a kiss. To die for *her* seemed like an entire life to me. In 1760 I fell in love with a Vendramini, a woman of eighteen, married to a Sagredo, one of the richest senators, a man of thirty who loved his wife madly. My sweetheart and I were as innocent as two cherubs when the *sposo** caught us speaking of love; I had no weapon, he missed me, I jumped on him, I strangled him with my two hands, wringing his neck like a chicken's. I wanted to go away with Bianca, she refused to come with me. There's women for you! I went away on my own, I was condemned, my property was sequestrated for the benefit of my heirs; but I had taken along my diamonds, five paintings by Titian, rolled up, and all of my gold. I went to Milan, where I wasn't bothered: my affair didn't interest the government in the least.

"One small observation before I go on," he said after a pause. "Whether or not a woman's fancies influence a child while she is carrying him or when she conceives him, it's a fact that my mother had a passion for gold during her pregnancy. I have a monomania for gold, the satisfaction of which is so necessary to my existence that, in every situation in which I've found myself, I've never been without some

---

*"Husband," in Italian.

gold on my person; I constantly handle gold; when young, I always wore jewelry and always had two or three hundred ducats on me."

Saying this, he took two ducats out of his pocket and showed them to me.

"I can sense gold. Although blind, I stop in front of jewelry shops. This passion ruined me; I became a gambler so I could stake gold. I wasn't a sharpster, I got outsharped, I was wiped out.

"When my fortune was gone, I was seized with the rage to see Bianca; I returned to Venice secretly, I found her again, I was happy for six months, hidden in her home, fed by her.

"I thought in my bliss I could live out my life that way. She was courted by the Provveditore;* he guessed he had a rival; in Italy men can sense it. He spied on us and caught us in bed, the coward! You can imagine how brisk our fight was: I didn't kill him, but wounded him badly.

"That adventure cut short my happiness. From that day on I never found a woman like Bianca again.

"I've had great pleasures. I've lived at the court of Louis XV among the most celebrated women; nowhere did I find the qualities, the grace, the love of my dear Venetian woman.

"The Provveditore had his people, he summoned them, the palace was surrounded, invaded; I defended myself so I could die before the eyes of Bianca, who helped me kill the Provveditore. Earlier that woman had refused to run away with me; but after six months of happiness she wanted to share my death, and she received several wounds. Caught in a large cloak that was thrown over me, I was rolled up in it, transported in a gondola, and taken to a dungeon in the Wells.† I was twenty-two, and I held onto the stump of my sword so tightly that, to get it, they would have had to cut off my hand.

"By a singular chance or, rather, inspired with a precautionary thought, I hid this piece of steel in a corner, as if I could make use of it. I was tended to. None of my wounds was mortal. At twenty-two a man gets over everything. I was due to be decapitated; I pretended to be ill in order to buy time. I thought I was in a dungeon near the canal; my plan was to escape by digging through the wall and swimming across the canal, at the risk of drowning. This is the reasoning on which my hopes were founded:

"Every time the jailer brought me food, I would read indications written on the walls, such as 'Palace Side,' 'Canal Side,' and 'Underground Side,' and I finally recognized in this an arrangement

---

*High administrative official in the Venetian Republic.
†The Pozzi, an infamous subterranean prison in the Palace of the Doges.

whose meaning hardly troubled me, but which was explainable by the current state of the ducal palace, which isn't completed.

"With the genius supplied by the desire to regain freedom, by feeling the surface of a stone with my fingertips, I succeeded in deciphering an Arabic inscription in which the engraver notified his successors that he had loosened two stones of the lowest course and had dug a tunnel eleven feet down. To continue his accomplishment, it was necessary to spread out on the very floor of the dungeon the pieces of stone and mortar produced by working on the excavation.

"Even if the guards or inquisitors hadn't been reassured by the solid construction of the building, which called for an outside surveillance only, the layout of the Wells, into which a few steps led down, made it possible to raise the ground level gradually without the guards' noticing.

"That immense effort had been for nought, at least for the man who had undertaken it, for its lack of completion indicated that the unknown man had died. For his dedication not to be wasted forever, it was necessary for a prisoner to know Arabic; but I had studied Eastern languages at the Armenian monastery. A sentence written behind the stone explained the fate of that unfortunate man, who died a victim to his enormous riches, which Venice had coveted and seized.

"It took me a month to achieve a result. While I was working, and in the moments when fatigue overwhelmed me, I could hear the sound of gold, I could see gold in front of me, I was dazzled by diamonds! Oh, wait!

"One night, my blunted steel struck on wood. I sharpened my sword stump and made a hole in that wood. To be able to work, I rolled onto my stomach like a snake, I stripped bare so I could work like a mole, stretching out my hands in front of me and supporting myself on the very stone. Two days before the day on which I was to appear before my judges, during the night, I decided on attempting one last effort; I pierced through the wood, and my steel found nothing beyond it. Imagine my surprise when I put my eyes to the hole! I was inside the paneling of a cellar in which a dim light allowed me to catch sight of a heap of gold. The Doge and one of the Council of Ten* were in that vault, I heard their voices; their conversation informed me that this was the secret treasury of the Republic, the gifts of the Doges, and the reserves of the booty known as the "Venice pence," a portion of the proceeds from their expeditions. I was saved! When the jailer came, I made him the proposition of allowing me to escape and joining me in making off with all we could carry. There was no cause to hesitate; he agreed.

---

*Consiglio dei Dieci, supreme governing body of the Venetian Republic.

"A ship was setting sail for the Levant, all precautions were taken, Bianca helped in taking the measures I dictated to my accomplice. So as not to arouse suspicions, Bianca was to rejoin us at Smyrna.

"In one night the hole was widened, and we went down into Venice's secret treasury.

"What a night! I saw four casks full of gold. In the anteroom, silver was likewise heaped up in two piles that left a path in the middle, to make it possible to cross the room; there coins were banked up five feet high along the walls. I thought the jailer would go mad; he was singing, jumping, laughing, skipping around in the gold; I threatened to strangle him if he wasted time or made noise. In his joy, he failed to notice at first a table that held the diamonds. I leapt onto it dexterously enough to fill up my sailor's jacket and trouser pockets. God, I didn't even take a third of them! Beneath that table were gold ingots.

"I persuaded my companion to fill up as many sacks of them as we could carry, informing him that that was the only way to escape being found out in foreign countries.

"'Pearls, jewels, and diamonds would cause us to be recognized,' I said to him.

"Greedy as we might be, we were only able to take two thousand pounds of gold, which necessitated six trips across the prison to the gondola. The sentinel at the water gate had been won over by means of a sack containing ten pounds of gold. As for the two gondoliers, they thought they were serving the Republic. At daylight we left.

"When we were out at sea, and I recalled that night; when I remembered my emotions; when I saw in my memory that immense treasury, in which, according to my calculations, I had left behind thirty million in silver and twenty million in gold, as well as several million in diamonds, pearls, and rubies, I experienced a kind of onset of madness. I had gold fever. We disembarked at Smyrna and immediately embarked for France. As we were boarding the French vessel, God did me the favor of ridding me of my accomplice. At that moment I wasn't thinking of the full import of that stroke of bad luck; in fact, I felt very happy about it.

"We were so completely unstrung that we remained in a daze and didn't talk to each other, waiting to be in safety so we could enjoy ourselves at our ease. It isn't surprising that that fellow lost his head. You'll see to what an extent God punished me. I didn't feel calm until I had sold two thirds of my diamonds in London and Amsterdam, and bought business shares with my gold dust.

"For five years I hid in Madrid; then, in 1770, I came to Paris under a Spanish name, and led an extremely brilliant life. Bianca had died.

"In the midst of my pleasures, while I was enjoying a fortune of six

million, I was struck blind. I have no doubt but that that infirmity was
the result of my stay in the dungeon and my digging through the stone,
unless my ability to see gold produced a strain on my vision that pre-
destined me to lose my sight.

"At that moment I was in love with a woman whose fate I hoped to
link with mine; I had told her the secret of my name. She belonged to
a powerful family; I derived all sorts of hopes from the favor with which
Louis XV looked on me. I had placed my confidence in that woman,
who was a friend of Madame du Barry; she advised me to consult a
well-known eye specialist in London; but, after living a few months in
that city, I was abandoned by that woman in Hyde Park; she had robbed
me of my entire fortune, leaving me without resources; for, being
obliged to conceal my name, which would expose me to the vengeance
of Venice, I was unable to call upon anyone's aid; I was afraid of Venice.

"My infirmity was exploited by the spies whom that woman had set
upon me.

"I spare you a number of adventures worthy of Gil Blas.*

"Your revolution arrived. I was compelled to enter the Quinze-
Vingts, where that creature had me admitted after having held me for
two years at Bicêtre as a madman; I was never able to kill her, I
couldn't see and I was too poor to hire an assassin. If, before losing
Benedetto Carpi, my jailer, I had consulted him as to the precise location of my dungeon, I would have been able to rediscover the treasure,
returning to Venice when the Republic was abolished by Napoleon.†

"And yet, in spite of my blindness, let's go to Venice! I'll find the
gate to the prison again, I'll see the gold through the walls, I'll sense it
beneath the waters where it's buried; for the events that have overturned the power of Venice are of such a nature that the secret of that
treasure must have died along with Vendramino, Bianca's brother, a
Doge who I hoped would have made peace between me and the
Council of Ten.

"I wrote notes to the First Consul,‡ I proposed a deal to the Emperor
of Austria, they all showed me the door as if I were a madman! Come,
let's set out for Venice, let's set out as beggars and come back as mil-
lionaires; we'll buy back my property and you'll be my heir, you'll be
prince of Varese."

Stunned by this confidence, which in my imagination was taking on
the proportions of an epic poem, at the sight of that white hair, and in

---

*Picaresque novel by Alain-René Le Sage, published between 1715 and 1735.
†After Napoleon abolished the Venetian Republic in 1797, Venice was an Austrian pos-
session until it became part of the Kingdom of Italy in 1866.
‡Napoleon's title during the time of the First Consulate (1799–1804).

view of the black water of the Bastille moat, a water as stagnant as that in the canals of Venice, I made no reply.

Facino Cane no doubt believed that I was judging him as all the others had, with a contemptuous pity; he made a gesture that expressed the entire philosophy of despair.

That narrative had carried him back, perhaps, to his happy days, to Venice: he grasped his clarinet and, in a melancholy way, played a Venetian song, a barcarolle, for which he regained his original talent, that of a patrician in love. It was something like the *Super flumina Babylonis.* My eyes filled with tears.

If a few belated strollers happened to be walking along the Boulevard Bourdon, they no doubt stopped to listen to that final prayer of the exile, the final regret for a lost name, in which was mingled the memory of Bianca.

But soon gold resumed the upper hand, and the fatal passion extinguished that gleam of youth.

"That treasure," he said to me, "I see it always, awake or in my dreams; I walk through it, the diamonds sparkle, I'm not as blind as you think: the gold and the diamonds illumine my night, the night of the last Facino Cane, for my title will be transferred to the Memmi clan. God! The punishment for the murderer began very early! *Ave Maria . . .*"

He recited a few prayers that I didn't hear.

"We'll go to Venice," I exclaimed when he rose.

"So I've found my man," he exclaimed, his face on fire.

I led him home on my arm; he shook my hand at the gate to the Quinze-Vingts, at the moment when some members of the wedding were going home and yelling at the top of their voices.

"Shall we leave tomorrow?" said the old man.

"As soon as we have some money."

"But we can go on foot, I'll beg for alms . . . I'm sturdy, and people are young when they see gold before them."

Facino Cane died during the winter after languishing two months. The poor man had caught a severe cold.

---

*"By the waters of Babylon" (Psalm 137).

A PASSION IN THE DESERT

1. Natural History of a Preternatural Story

"WHAT A frightening show!" she exclaimed upon leaving Martin's menagerie.

She had just been watching that bold enterprising showman "working" with his hyena, to use the language of advertising posters.

"In what way," she went on, "can he have tamed his animals so thoroughly that he's sure enough of their affection to . . ."

"That fact, which seems problematic to you," I interrupted her, "is nonetheless something quite natural . . ."

"Oh!" she cried, a smile of disbelief playing on her lips.

"So you think that animals are totally devoid of passions?" I asked. "Let me tell you that we can infect them with every vice endemic to our degree of civilization."

She looked at me with surprise.

"But," I resumed, "I admit that, when I first saw Martin, an exclamation of surprise escaped me, just as with you now. At the time, I was seated next to an army veteran, who had lost his right leg; he had come in along with me. I was struck by his appearance. He was one of those daredevils marked with the brand of war, who have Napoleon's battles written all over them. Most of all, that old soldier had a candid and cheerful look that I always find prepossessing. No doubt he was the kind of old trooper whom nothing catches off guard, who can find something to laugh about even while a comrade is dying beside him, who will bury him or ransack his body merrily, who faces up to cannonballs without flinching; in short, someone who doesn't take long to make up his mind and who would rub elbows with the devil. After studying the menagerie owner most attentively when he stepped out of the cage, my companion pursed his lips, so as to indicate mockery and contempt with that sort of meaningful sneer which superior men affect to set themselves apart from the gullible crowd. Thus, when I protested, insisting that Martin was a brave man, he smiled and, shaking his head, said with an air of competence: "Old hat!"

50

"What do you mean, 'old hat'?" I replied. "If you're willing to explain that mystery to me, I'll be much obliged to you."

A few minutes later, after we had introduced ourselves, we went to dine in the first restaurant we came across. When we got to dessert, a bottle of champagne totally refreshed that odd soldier's memory. He told me his story and I saw that he had been justified in calling out: "Old hat!"

2. A Woman's Curiosity

Back at her place, she wheedled me so and made me so many promises that I agreed to set down on paper what the soldier had told me in confidence. Thus, the next day she received this episode of an epic that might be called "The French in Egypt."

3. The Desert

During General Desaix's campaign in Upper Egypt, a Provençal soldier fell into the hands of the Maghribis* and was carried by those Arabs into the desert located beyond the cataracts of the Nile.

In order to put between themselves and the French army a distance sufficient to relieve them of worry, the Maghribis made a forced march, not stopping until nightfall. They camped around a well that was hidden by palm trees, near which they had previous buried some food supplies. Never imagining that their prisoner might get the idea of running away, they were content merely to tie his hands, and they all went to sleep after eating a few dates and giving their horses barley.

When the bold Provençal saw that his enemies were no longer able to guard him, he used his teeth to take hold of a scimitar; then, using his knees to keep the blade steady, he cut the cords that deprived him of the use of his hands, and he was free. He immediately seized a carbine and a dagger, provided himself with a supply of dried dates, a little bag of barley, gunpowder, and bullets; girded on a scimitar, mounted a horse, and lit out briskly in the direction where he imagined the French army to be.

Impatient to see a bivouac again, he spurred on the already weary horse so hard that the poor animal died, with its sides all ripped up, leaving the Frenchman in the middle of the desert.

After walking a while on the sand with all the courage of an escaped convict, the soldier was compelled to halt; the sun was going down. Despite the beauty of the night sky in the East, he didn't feel strong

---

*Name derived from Arabic word meaning "west, sunset," and thus connoting dwellers in the extreme west of the Islamic world—Tunisia, Algeria, and Morocco—but not in Egypt, as Balzac uses the term here.

enough to keep going. Fortunately he had been able to reach a rise at
the top of which a few palms stood straight and tall; their leaves, which
he had sighted some time before, had kindled the fondest hopes in his
heart. His weariness was so great that he lay down on a granite rock that
was whimsically shaped like an army cot, and dropped off without taking any precautions for his safety while asleep. He had thrown his life
away. In fact, his last thought was one of regret. He was already sorry
that he had left the Maghribis, whose nomadic life was beginning to
look good to him now that he was far from them and without aid.

He was awakened by the sun, whose pitiless beams, striking vertically
on the granite, made it unbearably hot. Now, the Provençal had committed the blunder of situating himself in the direction opposite to the
shade cast by the majestic green caps of the palm trees . . . He looked
at those solitary trees, and gave a start! They reminded him of the elegant shafts, crowned by long leaves, that characterize the Saracen
columns of the Arles cathedral. But when he had finished counting the
trees and he cast his eyes all around, the most fearful despair settled on
his soul. He saw a boundless ocean. The blackish sands of the desert extended in every direction as far as the eye could see, and they were
sparkling like a steel blade struck by a bright light. He didn't know
whether it was a sea of ice or a series of lakes smooth as a mirror. Borne
in waves, a fiery vapor eddied above that shifting terrain. The sky had
an Eastern brilliance of a heart-wrenching purity, which leaves nothing
to the imagination. The sky and the earth were ablaze. The silence was
frightening in its wild and awesome majesty. Infinity and immensity oppressed the soul on every side: not a cloud in the sky, not a breeze in
the air, no unevenness on the bosom of the sands, which were pat-
terned with tiny ripples; lastly, just as at sea in good weather, the horizon ended in a line of light as thin as the edge of a sword.

The Provençal hugged the trunk of one of the palms as if it were the
body of a friend; then, sheltered in the slender, straight shadow that the
tree cast on the granite, he started to weep; he sat down and remained
there, observing in deep dejection the merciless scene that met his eyes.
He called out as if to tempt the solitude. His voice, lost among the hollows
of the rise, produced a thin sound far off that awakened no echo; the echo
was in his heart: the Provençal was twenty-two, he loaded his carbine.

"Whenever the time comes!" he said to himself as he placed the
weapon of his deliverance on the ground.

4. The New Robinson Crusoe Finds an Unusual Friday

Looking back and forth between the blackish space and the blue space,
the soldier dreamed of France. He smelled with delight the gutters of

Paris, he recalled the cities he had passed through, the faces of his comrades, and the most insignificant events in his life. Finally, his Southern imagination soon made him believe he saw the stones of his dear Provence in the effects of the heat that floated over the outspread sheet of the desert.

Fearing all the dangers of that cruel mirage, he walked down the slope opposite to the one he had climbed up the day before. He was overjoyed to discover a kind of cave naturally hewn from the immense blocks of granite that formed the base of that hillock. The remains of a mat indicated that that refuge had once been inhabited. Then, a few steps further, he caught sight of palm trees laden with dates. Thereupon the instinct that keeps us alive was reawakened in his heart. He had hopes of living long enough to await the approach of some Maghribis, or perhaps he would soon hear the roar of cannons; for at that time Bonaparte was making his way across Egypt.

Revived by that thought, the Frenchman knocked down a few bunches of ripe fruit, under the weight of which the date palms seemed to be bending, and, when tasting that unexpected manna, he was sure that the inhabitant of the cave had cultivated the palms. Indeed, the fresh tasty flesh of the date testified to the pains taken by his predecessor. The Provençal suddenly veered from deep despair to almost delirious joy. He climbed back to the top of the hill and busied himself for the rest of the day in cutting down one of the infertile palm trees that had shaded him the day before. A vague recollection made him think about desert animals; and, foreseeing that they might come to drink at the spring that, hidden among the sands, emerged below the blocks of stone, he decided to protect himself from their visits by erecting a barrier at the door to his hermitage. Despite his zeal, despite the strength he derived from his fear of being devoured while sleeping, he was unable to cut up the palm tree into sections that day; but he managed to fell it. When, toward evening, that king of the desert toppled, the noise of the fall resounded far and wide; it was like a groan uttered by the solitude; it made the soldier shudder as if he had heard some voice predicting a disaster.

But, like an heir who doesn't mourn the death of his relative too long, he stripped that fine tree of the tall, wide green leaves that are its poetic ornament, and used them to repair the mat on which he was going to sleep.

Wearied by the heat and his labors, he fell asleep beneath the red ceiling of his damp cave. In the middle of the night his sleep was disturbed by an unusual sound. He sat up, and the deep silence that reigned allowed him to make out inhalations and exhalations of such wild force that they couldn't be those of a human being. A deep-seated fear, made even greater by the darkness, the silence, and his imaginings upon being awakened, turned his heart to ice. In fact, he hardly felt the painful crawling of his scalp when, by dilating the pupils of his eyes, he saw in the shadow two weak yellow lights. At first he attributed those lights to some reflection from his own pupils; but soon, the great brightness of the night gradually helping him to distinguish the objects that were located in the cave, he caught sight of an enormous animal lying two paces away from him. Was it a lion, a tiger, or a crocodile? The Provençal wasn't sufficiently educated to know under which subgenus to classify his enemy; but his fright was all the stronger because his ignorance made him imagine all sorts of disasters at once. He endured the cruel torture of listening, of perceiving the ups and downs of that breathing, without missing a beat of it, and without daring to make the slightest move. An odor as strong as the one emitted by foxes, but more piercing—heavier, so to speak—filled the cave; and, when the Provençal had got a whiff of it, his terror was at its height, for he could no longer call into question the existence of the dreadful companion whose royal den he was using as a bivouac. Soon the rays of the moon, which was hastening toward the horizon, illuminated the lair and cast an imperceptible glow on the spotted fur of a leopard.

That Egyptian kin of the lion was sleeping curled up like a big dog, the peaceful owner of a fancy doghouse at the gate to a townhouse; its eyes, opened for a moment, had shut again. Its face was turned toward the Frenchman.

A thousand muddled thoughts passed through the mind of the leopard's prisoner; at first, he wanted to kill it with a gunshot; but he observed that there wasn't enough space between him and it to take aim at it; the barrel would have extended beyond the animal. And what if he should awaken it? That possibility paralyzed him. Listening to his heart beat in the silence, he cursed the overloud beats that the rush of blood was creating, fearing to disturb that slumber which allowed him to look for some way to save his life. Twice he laid his hand on his scimitar with the purpose of cutting off his enemy's head; but the difficulty of cutting through short, coarse hair made him give up his bold plan.

"And if I missed? That would mean certain death," he thought.

He preferred to try his chances in a fight, and decided to wait until daybreak.

And day wasn't long in coming.

The Frenchman was then able to scrutinize the leopard; its muzzle was stained with blood.

"It's had a good meal!" he thought, without worrying whether the feast had consisted of human flesh. "It won't be hungry when it wakes up."

5. Do Animals Have a Soul?

It was a female. The fur on her stomach and thighs was gleaming white. Several small spots, like velvet, formed pretty bracelets around her paws. Her muscular tail was also white, but had black rings near the tip. The coat on her back and sides, yellow as dull gold, but very smooth and soft, bore those typical spots, grouped into rosettes, which distinguish leopards from the other species of the genus *Felis*.

This calm but frightening hostess was snoring in a pose as graceful as that of a cat lying on an ottoman cushion. Her bloodied paws, sinewy and well armed, were stretched out in front of her head, which was resting on them, and from which sprang those sparse straight whiskers which resemble silver wires. If, looking like that, she had been in a cage, the Provençal would surely have admired the animal's grace and the lively contrasts of the bright colors that lent her coat an imperial brilliance; but at that moment his sight was dimmed by that sinister appearance. The presence of the leopard, even asleep, made him experience the effect that the hypnotic eyes of a snake are said to have on a nightingale. The soldier's courage finally melted away for a moment in the face of that danger, whereas he would surely have been eager to face the mouth of cannons spewing grapeshot. Nevertheless, a brave thought awoke in his heart and dried up at its source the cold sweat that was pouring down his brow. Behaving like men who are pushed to the wall by misfortune but still defy death and lay themselves open to its blows, he saw, though not fully aware of it, that there was a tragedy being enacted in this adventure, and he resolved to play his part in it with honor down to the final scene.

"Wouldn't the Arabs have killed me the other day?" he said to himself.

Considering himself already dead, he waited bravely and with a nervous curiosity until his enemy awakened. When the sun appeared, the leopard suddenly opened her eyes; then she stretched out her paws violently, as if to rid them of their numbness and get all the stiffness out of them. Finally she yawned, showing her fearful dental equipment and her forked tongue, rough as a rasp.

"She's like a spoiled, elegant lady!" thought the Frenchman, seeing her curl up and make the gentlest, most coquettish movements.

She licked the blood that stained her paws and muzzle, and scratched her head with repeated gestures full of gracefulness.

"Good! Tidy up a little!" the Frenchman said to himself, regaining his good humor as his courage mounted. "We're going to wish each other good day."

And he took hold of the small, short dagger of which he had unburdened the Maghribis.

At that moment, the leopard turned her head toward the Frenchman and stared at him hard without moving forward. The rigidity of those metallic eyes and their intolerable brightness made the Provençal start, especially when the animal walked toward him; but he observed her in a fond way, and, looking her in the eye as if to hypnotize her, he let her approach him; then, with a motion just as gentle and loving as if he were about to caress the loveliest woman, he passed his hand along her whole body, from head to tail, scratching with his nails the flexible vertebrae that formed a ridge down the leopard's yellow back.

The animal lifted her tail voluptuously, her eyes suddenly became soft; and when, for the third time, the Frenchman bestowed those self-seeking caresses, she emitted one of those purrs with which our cats express their pleasure; but that murmur arose from a gullet so powerful and deep that it resounded in the cave like the last boomings of an organ in a church. The Provençal, understanding the importance of his caresses, multiplied them in a way that would bemuse and daze that imperious courtesan. When he felt sure he had quenched the ferocity of his capricious companion, whose hunger had been so fortunately assuaged the day before, he got up and tried to leave the cave; the leopard did let him go but, when he had climbed up the hill, she bounded with the lightness of sparrows hopping from branch to branch, and, coming up to the soldier, rubbed herself against his legs, arching her back like a housecat. Then, looking at her guest with eyes whose bright beams had become less rigid, she uttered that wild cry which naturalists compare to the sound of a saw.

"She's a demanding one!" exclaimed the Frenchman, with a smile.

He tried to play with her ears, to stroke her stomach, and scratch her head hard with his nails. And, noticing his success, he tickled the top of her head with the point of his dagger, watching for the right opportunity to kill her; but the hardness of the bones made him fearful of not succeeding.

The sultana of the desert showed her appreciation of her slave's talents by raising her head, stretching out her neck, and manifesting her state of intoxication by the calmness of her behavior. The Frenchman suddenly realized that, to kill that fierce princess at one blow, it was necessary to stab her in the throat, and he was raising his blade when the leopard, no doubt satiated, lay down gracefully at his feet, from time to time casting glances in which, despite an inborn harshness, some benevolent feeling was confusedly depicted.

The poor Provençal ate his dates, leaning against one of the palm trees; but, by turns, he darted a scrutinizing eye now over the desert in search of liberators, and now over his terrifying companion to see how constant her clemency would be. The leopard watched the place where the date kernels fell each time he threw one away, and at those moments her eyes expressed an incredible lack of trust. She was examining the Frenchman with a businessman's caution; but the examination came out in his favor, because, when he had finished his frugal meal, she licked his shoes and, with her strong, rough tongue, miraculously removed the dust that was encrusted in their creases.

"But when she gets hungry?" thought the Provençal.

6. The Provençal's Idea

Despite the shudder that his idea gave him, the soldier began measuring carefully the dimensions of the leopard, who was surely one of the most beautiful specimens of her species, for she was three feet tall and four feet long, not counting her tail. That powerful weapon, as round as a cudgel, was nearly three feet long. Her head, as large as that of a lioness, was distinguished by an unusual expression of shrewdness; the cold cruelty of tigers was its dominant feature, but it also had a vague resemblance to the face of a calculating woman. In short, the face of that solitary queen revealed at that moment a sort of good humor like that of Nero when he was drunk: she had slaked her thirst in blood and wanted to play.

The soldier made the experiment of walking to and fro; the leopard left him alone, contenting herself with watching him constantly, thus acting not so much like a faithful dog as like a fat Angora cat nervous over everything, even her master's movements. When he turned around, he saw, in the direction of the spring, the remains of his horse; the leopard had dragged its carcass all the way there. About two thirds of it was consumed. That sight reassured the Frenchman. It was easy for him then to explain the leopard's absence and the way she had spared him while he was sleeping.

That first good fortune emboldening him to see what the future would bring, he conceived the foolhardy hope of keeping on good terms with the leopard all day long, omitting no chance of taming her and getting into her good graces. He returned to her side and had the unutterable happiness to see her wave her tail almost imperceptibly. Then he sat down next to her without fear, and they started playing together; he took hold of her paws, her muzzle; he twisted her ears, turned her over on her back, and scratched her hot, silky sides hard. She let him do so, and when the soldier went to smooth the hair on her paws, she carefully drew in her claws, which were curved like Damascene blades. The Frenchman, who kept a hand on his dagger, still thought about plunging it into the belly of the overconfident leopard; but he was afraid of being throttled immediately as she thrashed about in her last throes. Besides, he heard in his heart something like remorse, calling out to him to spare a creature that was doing him no harm. It seemed to him he had found a friend in that boundless waste.

Involuntarily he recalled his first mistress, whom he had euphemistically nicknamed "Sweetie" because she was horribly jealous and because, the whole time their passion lasted, he had had to be on guard against the knife she constantly threatened him with. That memory of his earlier youth prompted him to try making the young leopard answer to that name, now that, with less fear, he was admiring her agility, grace, and softness.

Toward the end of the day, he had taken full stock of his perilous situation, and he almost enjoyed the anguish it entailed. Finally, his companion had at last grown accustomed to looking at him when he called out "Sweetie" in falsetto tones.

At sunset, Sweetie repeatedly uttered a deep, melancholy cry.

"She's well brought up!" thought the merry soldier. "She's saying her prayers!"

But that silent joke only occurred to him after he had observed the peaceful attitude that his comrade maintained.

"Go ahead, blondie dear, I'll let you go to bed first," he said, trusting to the power of his legs to escape as quickly as possible, once she was asleep, and to find another lodging during the night.

7. A Favor Such as Shopgirls Grant

The soldier awaited the time for his escape impatiently, and when it came, he walked vigorously in the direction of the Nile; but he had covered scarcely a quarter of a league over the sand when he heard the leopard bounding after him, uttering at intervals that sawlike sound which was even more terrifying than the dull thuds of her bounds.

"Well, well!" he said to himself, "she's taken a liking to me! . . . maybe this young leopard has never met anyone before; it's flattering to be the first one she's loved!"

At that moment the Frenchman fell into one of those patches of quicksand, so hazardous to travelers, from which it's impossible to escape. Feeling himself held fast, he cried out in alarm; the leopard seized him by the collar with her teeth, and, leaping back vigorously, drew him out of the pit as if by magic.

"Oh, Sweetie," exclaimed the soldier, patting her enthusiastically, "we're friends for life now. But no tricks, you hear?"

And he retraced his steps.

From that time on, it was as if the desert were inhabited. It contained a being to which the Frenchman could talk, one whose ferocity had softened where he was concerned, even though he couldn't find the reasons for that unbelievable friendship. Despite the strength of the soldier's desire to keep on his feet and on guard, he fell asleep. When he awoke, he no longer saw Sweetie; he climbed the hill and, in the distance, he caught sight of her bounding toward him, as is the wont of those animals, which are prevented from running by the extreme flexibility of their spine. Sweetie arrived with bloodied chops; she accepted the necessary caresses of her companion, even showing how happy they made her with some rumbling purrs. Her eyes, full of indolence, turned toward the Provençal with even more gentleness than the day before, as he spoke to her as if she were a pet.

"Oh, ho, miss, for you are a respectable girl, aren't you? See that? . . . We like to be cuddled. Aren't you ashamed? Did you eat some Maghribi?—Good! They're animals like you, anyhow! . . . But don't go gobbling up Frenchmen, will you? . . . I wouldn't love you any more!"

She played like a puppy with its master, allowing herself to be curled up, struck, and petted in turns; and at times she egged the soldier on, stretching out a paw and touching him with an entreating gesture.

8. Sweetie, Untalkative but Loyal

A few days went by in that manner.

This company allowed the Provençal to admire the sublime beauties of the desert. From the moment when he found in it hours of fear and calm, nourishment, and a creature to occupy his thoughts, his soul was agitated by contrasts . . . It was a life full of opposing elements. The solitude revealed all its secrets to him, enveloped him in its charms. In the rising and setting of the sun he discovered sights unknown to the world. He learned to give a start when hearing above his head the soft rustling of a bird's wings—a rare passerby!—when seeing the clouds mingle together—changeable and colorful travelers! At night he studied the effects of the moon on the ocean of sand, on which the simoom created waves, ripples, and swift changes. He lived with the Eastern day, admiring its wonderful displays; and often, after enjoying the fearsome spectacle of a sandstorm on that plain where the blown sand created dry, red fogs, death-dealing clouds, he watched the approach of the night with delight, for it was then that beneficent coolness fell from the stars. He listened to imaginary music in the sky. Then the solitude taught him to enjoy the treasures of daydreams. He would spend whole hours recalling trifles, comparing his past life with his present existence.

Finally he conceived a passion for his leopard, for he certainly needed some affection.

Whether it was because his will, powerfully projected, had altered his companion's nature, or because she found plenty to eat thanks to the battles then being fought in the desert, she spared the life of the Frenchman, who finally lost his mistrust, seeing her so tame.

He spent most of his time sleeping; but he was compelled at intervals to stay awake, like a spider at the center of its web, so as not to miss the moment when he would be delivered, if someone passed by within the circle of the horizon. He had sacrificed his shirt to make a flag, hoisted at the top of a palm tree he had stripped of its leaves. Counseled by necessity, he managed to keep it unfurled by holding it firm with sticks, because the wind might not be blowing it at the moment when the hoped-for traveler was looking at the desert.

It was during the long hours in which he abandoned hope that he amused himself with the leopard. Eventually he had come to know the various inflections of her voice, the expressions in her eyes; he had studied the capricious patterns of all the spots that adorned the gold of her coat. Sweetie no longer growled even when he took hold of the tuft of hair at the end of her mighty tail, to count its black and white rings, a graceful ornament that gleamed at a distance in the sun like gems. He took pleasure in contemplating her fine, velvety contours, the whiteness of her belly, the grace of her head. But it was especially when she frisked about that he contemplated her with greatest satisfaction, and the agility and youthfulness of her movements always surprised him; he admired her suppleness when she started to bound, creep, slide, crawl into tight places, catch hold of things, curl up, snuggle, dart about everywhere. However rapid her motion, however slippery a block of granite might be, she would stop short on it at the word "Sweetie."

One day, when the sun was blazing, an immense bird hovered in the air. The Provençal abandoned his leopard to examine this new guest; but, after waiting a moment, the deserted sultana gave a low growl.

"Devil take me, I believe she's jealous!" he exclaimed, seeing that her eyes had become rigid again. "Virginie's soul has entered that body, I'm sure of it!"

The eagle disappeared into the sky while the soldier admired the leopard's rounded rump. But there was so much grace and youth in her outlines! She was pretty as a woman. The blonde fur of her coat blended by subtle gradations into the tones of dull white that characterized her thighs. The light voluminously shed by the sun made that living gold, those brown spots, shine, lending them an indefinable attractiveness.

The Provençal and the leopard looked at each other knowingly; the coquette gave a start when she felt her friend's fingernails scratching the top of her head; her eyes gleamed like two lightning flashes, then she shut them tight.

"She has a soul," he said, observing the tranquillity of that queen of the sands, golden like them, white like them, solitary and burning like them . . .

9. A Misunderstanding

"Well," she said to me, "I've read your speech in defense of animals, but how did two persons so well suited to get along together finally end up?"

"Ah, there you have it! . . . They ended up the way all great passions end up, with a misunderstanding. Both parties believe they've been betrayed somehow, and they don't talk things through out of pride, they quarrel out of stubbornness."

"And sometimes just when everything is going beautifully," she said; "one look, one remark is enough. Well, will you finish the story?"

"It's extremely difficult, but you'll understand what the old trooper had already told me in confidence when, finishing his bottle of champagne, he exclaimed: 'I don't know what harm I did her, but she turned around as if she'd gone crazy; and, with her sharp teeth she bit into my thigh—with very little force, I'm sure. Thinking she wanted to eat me, I plunged my dagger into her neck. She rolled over, uttering a cry that chilled my heart; I saw her thrashing around as she looked at me without anger. I would have given everything in the world, even my decoration, which I didn't have yet, to bring her back to life. It was as if I had murdered a human being. And the soldiers who had seen my flag, and who came up to help me, found me bathed in tears . . . Well, sir,' he resumed after a moment of silence, 'since then I've been in wars in Germany, Spain, Russia, and France; I've carted my carcass all over, but I've never seen anything else like the desert . . . Oh, *that* is really beautiful.' 'What were your feelings there?' I asked. 'Oh, it can't be expressed, young man. Anyway, I don't miss my clump of palms and my leopard all the time . . . I have to be sad for that to happen. In the desert, you see, there's everything and there's nothing . . .' 'But can't you explain it to me?' 'Well,' he went on, with a gesture of impatience, 'it's God without people . . .'"

THE REVOLUTIONARY CONSCRIPT

TO MY DEAR ALBERT MARCHAND DE LA RIBELLERIE. Tours, 1836.

At times they saw him, by a phenomenon of vision or locomotion, abolish
space in its two modes of Time and Distance, of which one is mental and the
other physical. (*Louis Lambert*)*

ON A NOVEMBER evening in 1793, the leading citizens of Carentan
were in the salon of Madame de Dey, in whose home an "assembly"
was held daily. A few circumstances that wouldn't have attracted
attention in a big city, but were bound to preoccupy a small town enor-
mously, lent that customary gathering unusual interest. Two days earlier, Madame de Dey had closed her door to society, and had still
begged off from receiving on the following day, claiming that she was
feeling unwell. Even in ordinary times these two events would have
had the same effect in Carentan as a closing of all theaters in Paris. On
days like that, existence is somehow incomplete. But in 1793 Madame
de Dey's conduct could have the most baleful results. At that time the
slightest activity ventured by the nobility almost always became a matter of life or death for them. To understand fully the lively curiosity and
narrow-mindedly shrewd guesses that enlivened the Norman faces† of
all those people that evening, but especially to share in Madame de
Dey's secret dilemma, it is necessary to explain the role she played in
Carentan. The critical situation in which she found herself at that moment having no doubt been shared by many people during the
Revolution, the fellow-feeling of many a reader will complete the
fleshing-out of this narrative.

---

*Another work by Balzac, highly autobiographical and fantastic at one and the same
time.
†The natives of Normandy are proverbially depicted by their fellow French as cunning
and devious.

Madame de Dey, widow of a lieutenant general who had been knight of various orders, had left the royal court at the outset of the emigration. Possessing considerable property in the neighborhood of Carentan, she had taken refuge there, hoping that the influence of the Terror would be little felt there. This reasoning, based on a precise acquaintance with the area, was correct. The Revolution caused little damage in Lower Normandy. Although in the past Madame de Dey had seen only the noble families of the vicinity whenever she came to visit her lands, from political considerations she had now opened her doors to the town's leading middle-class citizens and to the new authorities, doing her best to make them proud of having conquered her, without arousing either hatred or jealousy among them. Gracious and kind, endowed with that ineffable sweetness which can please without recourse to self-abasement or entreaty, she had succeeded in winning general esteem by means of her exquisite tact, whose wise counsel allowed her to toe a delicate line and satisfy the demands of this hybrid society without humbling the touchy amour-propre of the parvenus or shocking that of her old friends.

About thirty-eight, she still retained, not that rosy, well-fed beauty which characterizes the girls of Lower Normandy, but a slender and, so to speak, aristocratic beauty. Her features were fine and delicate, her figure was thin and supple. When she spoke, her pale face seemed to light up and take on life. Her large, dark eyes were full of affability, but their calm, religious expression seemed to indicate that the basis for her existence was no longer located within herself. She had been wed at a very young age to an old, jealous soldier; the falseness of her position in a court given over to lovemaking surely aided greatly in casting a veil of grave melancholy over a face in which the charms and vivacity of love must once have shone. Since she was constantly compelled to repress those simple impulses, the emotions of a woman who still lives by her feelings, not her reflections, at the bottom of her heart she was still virginal where strong passions were concerned. Therefore, her principal charm was a result of that deep-seated youthfulness which her features sometimes revealed, and which lent her thoughts an innocent expression of desire. Her appearance commanded reserve, but in her bearing, in her voice, there was always an impetus toward an unknown future, as if she were still a young girl; soon even the coldest man found himself in love with her, and yet maintained a sort of respectful shyness, thanks to her polished manners, which kept him at a distance. Her soul, intrinsically lofty, but strengthened by bitter struggles, seemed to be too far beyond the commonplace, and the men around her felt unequal to the challenge. That soul definitely had need of a great passion. And so Madame de Dey's affections had centered on a single kind of love: maternal love. The happiness and pleasures she had been deprived of as a woman and wife she rediscovered in the excessive love she bore for her son. She loved him not only with a mother's pure and deep devotion, but also with a sweetheart's coquetry, with a wife's jealousy. She was unhappy when far from him, worried when he was away; she could never see enough of him; she lived only in him and for him. In order to make men understand the strength of this feeling, it will suffice to add that that son was not merely Madame de Dey's only child, but also her last surviving relative, the only being to whom she could link the fears, hopes, and joys of her life. The late Comte de Dey had been the last descendant of his family, just as she was sole heir of hers. Thus human calculations and interests had joined forces with the noblest needs of the soul to heighten in the countess' heart a feeling that is already so strong in women. She had had infinite trouble raising her son, and this had made him even more precious to her; twenty times, doctors had predicted his death; but, trusting to her presentiments and hopes, she had had the inexpressible joy of seeing him negotiate the perils of childhood successfully and of admiring the improvements in his constitution, in despite of the medical profession's pronouncements.

Thanks to unremitting care, that son had grown up and had developed so gracefully that, at twenty, he was counted as one of the most accomplished cavaliers at Versailles. Lastly, through a good fortune that doesn't always reward a mother's efforts, she was worshipped by her son; their souls were united by a fraternal fellow-feeling. If they hadn't been already joined to each other at the desire of nature, they would have instinctively felt for each other that man-to-man friendship so rarely found in life. Appointed second lieutenant of dragoons at eighteen, the young count had obeyed that era's conception of honor by following the princes into emigration.

Thus Madame de Dey, a noblewoman, wealthy, and the mother of an émigré, was fully aware of the dangers of her cruel situation. With no other desire than to preserve her great fortune for her son, she had renounced the happiness of accompanying him; but, when she read the rigorous laws by which the Republic was daily confiscating the property of émigrés in Carentan, she applauded herself for that act of courage. Wasn't she holding on to her son's treasures at the risk of her life? Then, upon hearing of the terrible executions ordered by the Convention, she went to bed each night happy in the knowledge that her only wealth was in safety, far from the dangers, far from the scaffolds. She was pleased to believe that she had chosen the best course to save all her wealth, of every sort, at the same time. Making the concessions to that secret goal that were demanded by the misfortunes of the era, but compromising neither

her womanly dignity nor her aristocratic code, she cloaked her sorrow in cool mystery. She had understood the difficulties that awaited her in Carentan. Coming there and taking her place at the top of the social ladder, wasn't that a daily defiance of the scaffold? But, upheld by a mother's courage, she was able to gain the affection of the poor by alleviating all cases of poverty indiscriminately, and made herself necessary to the rich by providing pleasure for them. She entertained the *procureur** of the commune, the mayor, the chief district judge, the public prosecutor, and even the judges of the revolutionary tribunal. The first four of the abovementioned, being unmarried, were courting her in hopes of winning her hand, either by frightening her with the harm they could do her or by offering her their protection. The public prosecutor, formerly a procurator in Caen, who had once taken care of the countess' business affairs, tried to make her love him by showing himself full of devotion and noble feelings: a shrewd scheme that had its dangers! He was the most to be dreaded among all her suitors. He alone knew thoroughly the amount of his former client's considerable fortune. His passion must have been fueled by all the greedy desires that could find support in a boundless power, his right to pronounce life or death in the district. This man, still young, injected so much nobility into his methods that Madame de Dey had not yet been able to see through him. But, scorning the danger involved in trying to outsmart Normans, she made use of the inventive wit and cunning with which nature has endowed women to play off the rival suitors against one another. By buying time she hoped to arrive safe and sound at the end of this turbulent period. At that time, the royalists still in France were deluded daily that they'd see the end of the Revolution the next day; and that belief was the ruin of many of them.

Despite these obstacles, the countess had quite skillfully kept her independence up to the day when, through an inexplicable imprudence, she had taken it into her head to close her doors. She generally inspired such a profound and genuine interest that the persons who had come to her home that first evening became seriously worried on learning she found it impossible to receive them; then, with that unconcealed curiosity which is an integral part of provincial customs, they asked about the misfortune, grief, or illness that must be afflicting Madame de Dey. To these questions an old housekeeper, whose name was Brigitte, replied that her mistress had shut herself in her room and didn't wish to see anybody, not even the members of her household. The existence, somewhat monastic, that the inhabitants of a small town lead creates in them a habit of analyzing and accounting for other

---

*Full form of this title, *procureur-syndic*; official responsible for enforcing the decisions of the local legislative assembly.

people's doings so insurmountable by nature that, after expressing sympathy for Madame de Dey, without knowing if she was really happy or sad, each of them began tracing the reasons for her sudden withdrawal.

"If she were ill," said the first curious one, "she would have sent for the doctor; but the doctor stayed at my place all day playing chess. He said to me, laughing, that, with times as they are, there's only one sickness . . . and that it's unfortunately incurable."

That joke was ventured cautiously. Then women, men, old codgers, and young girls started to scour the vast field of conjectures. Each one thought he could espy a secret, and that secret worked on everyone's imagination. The next day, their suspicions became malicious. Since everyone's life is an open book in a small town, the women were the first to learn that Brigitte had bought more provisions than usual in the market. This was an undeniable fact. Brigitte had been seen in the market square early in the morning and, quite surprisingly, had bought the only available hare. The whole town knew that Madame de Dey didn't like game. The hare became a point of departure for infinite suppositions. While taking their regular walk, the old men observed in the countess' house a sort of concerted activity that was revealed by the very precautions the servants took to conceal it. The valet was beating a carpet in the garden; the day before, no one would have paid any mind to that, but now that carpet became supporting evidence for the stories everyone was concocting. Everybody had his own. On that second day, learning that Madame de Dey had announced she was unwell, the leading citizens of Carentan met in the evening at the home of the mayor's brother, an old, married wholesale merchant, an honest and widely respected man to whom the countess showed a great deal of consideration. There, all the aspirants to the rich widow's hand had a more or less believable story to tell; and each of them was thinking how to turn to his own advantage the secret circumstance that compelled her to compromise herself in that way. The public prosecutor imagined a complicated plot for bringing Madame de Dey's son into her house at night. The mayor believed that a nonjuring priest, coming from Vendée,* had asked her for asylum; but the purchase of the hare, and on a Friday, made that theory very shaky. The chief district judge was strongly in favor of a Chouan† or Vendéen leader who was being hotly pursued. Others voted for a nobleman who had escaped from a Parisian prison. In short, everyone suspected the countess of being guilty of one of those generous actions that the laws of the day branded as a crime, one that could lead her to the scaffold. Moreover, the public prosecutor said in a low voice that they had to keep quiet and try to save the unfortunate woman from the precipice which she was approaching with rapid strides.

---

*For "nonjuring priest" and "Vendée," see notes to "An Episode During the Terror."
†The Chouans were anti-Revolution peasant guerrillas in the west of France.

"If you let this matter get around," he added, "I shall be compelled to step in, search her house, and then! . . ." He didn't finish, but everyone understood that reticence.

The countess' devoted friends were so alarmed for her sake that, on the morning of the third day, the *procureur* had his wife write her a note urging her to entertain as usual that evening. The old merchant, who was bolder, presented himself at Madame de Dey's home during the morning. Bolstered by the knowledge that he intended doing her a service, he demanded to be shown in to see her, and was dumbfounded to catch sight of her in the garden, busy cutting the last flowers from her beds to decorate vases with them.

"No doubt she's offering asylum to a lover," the old man said to himself, seized with pity for that charming woman. The old expression on the countess' face made him sure that his suspicions were correct. Deeply stirred by this devotion, which is natural in women but always touches our heart, because all men are flattered when a woman makes a sacrifice for any individual man, the merchant informed the countess of the rumors flying around the town and the danger she was in. "For," he said in conclusion, "if some of our officials are quite ready to forgive you for a heroic act on behalf of a priest, no one will pity you if they discover you're sacrificing yourself for an affair of the heart."

At these words, Madame de Dey looked at the old man with an air of bewilderment and irrationality that made him shudder, old as he was.

"Come," she said, taking him by the hand and leading him to her bedroom, where, after making sure they were alone, she drew from her bosom a dirty, crumpled letter. "Read this," she cried, making a violent effort to utter the words.

She fell into her armchair as if prostrate with exhaustion. While the old merchant was looking for his glasses and cleaning them, she raised her eyes in his direction, studied him curiously for the first time, then, in a shaky voice, said softly: "I'm putting myself in your hands."

"Am I not participating in your crime?" the good man replied matter-of-factly.

She started. For the first time, in that small town, her soul was attuned to someone else's. The old merchant suddenly understood both the depression and the joy of the countess. Her son had taken part in the expedition to Granville;* he was writing to his mother from the depths of his prison, holding out a sad and sweet hope to her. Having no doubt he would be able to escape, he announced a period of three

---

*A town not far from Carentan attacked by the Vendéens in 1793. Apparently Madame de Dey's son had not emigrated to Germany, as had many other nobles, but to the west of France.

days in the course of which he was to show up at her house in disguise. The fatal letter contained heart-rending farewells in case he wasn't in Carentan by the evening of the third day, and he asked his mother to hand over quite a large sum to the messenger who had agreed to bring her that dispatch in the face of a thousand dangers. The paper shook in the old man's hands.

"And this is the third day," cried Madame de Dey, who rose rapidly, took back the letter, and started pacing.

"You've done imprudent things," said the merchant. "Why did you buy provisions?"

"But he may arrive starving, worn out with fatigue, and . . ." She didn't finish.

"I can count on my brother," resumed the old man. "I'm going to make him cooperate with you."

On this occasion the merchant regained the shrewdness he had formerly exercised in his business dealings, and he gave her advice that was full of prudence and wisdom. After they had agreed on everything each of them was to say and do, the old man, finding clever pretexts, visited the leading homes in Carentan, announcing that Madame de Dey, whom he had just seen, would be entertaining that evening, despite her poor health. Pitting his wits against Norman cunning during the interrogation each family put him through concerning the nature of the countess' illness, he managed to deceive almost everyone who was interested in that mysterious affair. His first visit worked wonders. To an old, gout-ridden lady he recounted that Madame de Dey had almost died from an attack of gout on the stomach; the celebrated Tronchin once having instructed her, whenever the same problem occurred, to place on her chest the skin of a hare that had been flayed alive, and to stay in bed without making the slightest move, the countess, in mortal danger two days earlier, was now, after religiously following Tronchin's peculiar prescription, far enough recovered to entertain visitors to her house that evening. This yarn was amazingly effective, and the Carentan doctor, a royalist at heart, increased its success by the pompous way in which he discussed the remedy. Nevertheless, suspicions had taken root too deeply in the mind of a few stubborn or philosophical people to be entirely eliminated; so that, in the evening, those admitted to Madame de Dey's home arrived there eagerly and early, some to observe her behavior, the others out of friendship, and most of them affected by the miraculous nature of her recovery. They found the countess seated at the corner of the large fireplace in her salon, which was almost as plain as the others in Carentan; for, to avoid wounding her guests' narrow minds, she had decided to do without the luxurious pleasures she had formerly been accustomed to, and had made no changes in her house. The tile floor of the reception room wasn't even polished. She left the dark old tapestries on the walls, kept the local furniture, used tallow candles, and followed the town's customs, adopting provincial life without shrinking from the hardest-to-bear pettiness or the most unpleasant privations. But, knowing that her guests would forgive her for extravagance intended for their own well-being, she neglected nothing when it came to supplying them with personal pleasures. Thus, she gave them excellent dinners. She went so far as to feign avarice so as to please those calculating minds; and, after being skillful enough to allow them to wring some concessions out of her in the way of luxuries, she knew how to obey them gracefully. Thus, about seven in the evening, the best bad company in Carentan was in her home, forming a wide circle in front of the fireplace. The lady of the house, supported in her misfortune by the compassionate glances that the old merchant cast at her, submitted with matchless courage to the detailed questions and the frivolous and stupid discourses of her guests. But each time she heard her door knocker, or each time she heard steps on the street, she hid her emotions, raising questions that were of monetary interest to the community. She initiated noisy arguments about the quality of various ciders, and was so well seconded by her confidant that the gathering nearly forgot to spy on her, finding her behavior natural and her self-control unshakable. The public prosecutor and one of the judges of the revolutionary tribunal remained silent, attentively observing the slightest expressions on her face and listening for sounds in the house, despite the hubbub; on several occasions, they asked her embarrassing questions, to which the countess nevertheless replied with admirable presence of mind. Mothers have such courage! After Madame de Dey had organized the card games, placing everyone at tables for boston, reversi, or whist, she remained a while longer chatting with some young people with extreme unconstraint, playing her part like a consummate actress. She got someone to ask her for a set of lotto, claimed she was the only one who knew where it was, and vanished.

"I'm choking to death, poor Brigitte," she exclaimed, wiping away tears that flowed freely from her eyes, which shone with fever, sorrow, and impatience. "He just doesn't come," she continued, looking at the room which she had entered. "Here I can breathe and go on living. Just a few more minutes, though, and he'll be here! For he's still alive, I'm sure. My heart tells me so. Don't you hear anything, Brigitte? Oh, I'd give the rest of my life to know whether he's in prison or if he's walking across country! I wish I could stop thinking."

Once more she examined the quarters to see if everything was in order. A good fire was burning in the fireplace; the shutters were carefully closed; the furniture was so clean, it shone; the way the bed was made proved that the countess, along with Brigitte, had seen to the slightest details; and her hopes were revealed by the tender care that seemed to have been taken with that room, in which the fragrance emitted by the flowers bespoke the gracious sweetness of love and its most chaste caresses. Only a mother could have foreseen a soldier's wants and have prepared everything to satisfy them so completely. A delicious meal, choice wines, footwear, linens; in short, everything that might be needful or pleasing to a weary traveler was assembled so that he would lack for nothing, so that the delights of home would show him how a mother could love.

"Brigitte?" said the countess in a heart-rending tone of voice as she went to place a chair in front of the table, as if to make her wishes come true, as if to increase the strength of her illusions.

"Oh, madame, he'll come. He's not far away.—I'm sure he's alive and on the way," Brigitte continued. "I put a key in the Bible and held it on my fingers while Cottin* was reading the Gospel of Saint John . . . and, madame, the key didn't turn!"

"Is that a sure sign?" asked the countess.

"Oh, madame, everyone knows it is. I'd wager my salvation that he's still alive. God can't make a mistake."

"Despite the danger that awaits him here, I would still like to see him with us."

"Poor Monsieur Auguste!" cried Brigitte. "He must be on foot, walking along the roads."

"And here are the church bells ringing eight o'clock," cried the countess in terror.

She was afraid she had tarried longer than she ought in that room where she could believe her son was alive, seeing everything that bore witness to his life. She went downstairs; but, before entering the salon, she stopped for a moment below the staircase colonnade, listening to hear whether any sound was awakening the silent echoes of the town. She smiled at Brigitte's husband, who was acting as sentinel and whose eyes seemed dazed after he had given so much attention to the murmurs of the town square and the night. She saw her son in all things everywhere. Soon she returned to the salon, putting on a cheerful appearance, and started playing lotto with some little girls; but, from time to time, she complained of feeling unwell, and went back to sit in her armchair near the fireplace.

That is how things stood and what was on people's minds in Madame de Dey's home, while, on the road from Paris to Cherbourg

*Brigitte's husband, another servant.

a young man wearing a brown carmagnole, an obligatory garment at that time, was heading for Carentan. When the levies were just beginning, there was little discipline, if any. The needs of the moment hardly permitted the Republic to outfit its soldiers immediately, and it wasn't unusual to see the roads covered with conscripts who still had on their civilian clothing. These young men would reach their halting places before the rest of their battalion, or would fall behind, since their progress depended on how well they could endure the fatigue of a long march. The traveler of whom we are speaking was far in advance of the column of conscripts who were heading for Cherbourg, and whom the mayor of Carentan was expecting at any hour, so he could give them their billeting orders. This young man was walking with steps that were heavy but still firm, and his bearing seemed to indicate that he had been familiar for some time with the rigors of army life. Even though the moon was illuminating the meadows bordering on Carentan, he had noticed large white clouds ready to dump snow onto the countryside; and the fear of being caught in a blizzard no doubt lent urgency to his gait, which at the moment was livelier than his weariness could stand. On his back was a nearly empty rucksack, and in his hand he held a boxwood walking stick that he had cut from the high, wide hedges formed by that shrub around most of the estates in Lower Normandy. This solitary traveler entered Carentan, whose towers, edged with eerie gleams of moonlight, had come into sight a while before. His footsteps awakened the echoes of the silent streets, in which he came across no one; he was compelled to ask a weaver who was still working where the mayor's house was. That official lived a short distance away, and the conscript was soon sheltered in the porch of the mayor's house, where he sat down on a stone bench to await the billeting order he had requested. But, called inside by that official, he appeared before him and became the object of a careful scrutiny. The infantryman was a young man of pleasing appearance who seemed to belong to a distinguished family. His attitude bespoke nobility. The intelligence that a good education imparts was clearly to be seen on his face.

"What's your name?" asked the mayor, casting a very shrewd glance at him.

"Julien Jussieu," answered the conscript.

"And you come from?" said the official, showing a smile of disbelief.
"From Paris."

"Your comrades must be far away," the Norman continued, in a sarcastic tone.

"I'm three leagues ahead of the battalion."

"Some strong feeling must surely bring you to Carentan, citizen conscript?" said the mayor with a shrewd expression. "It's all right," he added, enjoining silence with a gesture of his hand on the young man, who was ready to speak; "we know where to send you. Here," he added, handing him his billeting order, "get along with you, *Citizen Jussieu!*"

A touch of irony was to be heard in the way the official uttered the last two words, as he held out an order on which Madame de Dey's address was written. The young man read the address with an air of curiosity.

"He knows very well he doesn't have far to go. And when he's outside, it won't take him long to cross the square!" exclaimed the mayor to himself as the young man left. "He's really brave, my God guide him! He's got an answer for everything. Yes, but if someone other than I had asked to see his papers, he would have been done for!"

At that moment the Carentan bells had rung nine-thirty; the lanterns were being lit in Madame de Dey's vestibule; the servants were helping their masters and mistresses on with their clogs, greatcoats, or mantelets; the cardplayers had settled their accounts, and were preparing to leave all together, in accordance with the established custom in every small town.

"It looks as if the prosecutor wants to stay," said a lady, noticing that that significant person was missing when they all separated on the square, each couple heading for home after exhausting all the good-night formulas.

That fearsome official was in fact alone with the countess, who, all atremble, was waiting for him to decide to go.

"Citizen," he said at last after a long silence that was somewhat frightening, "I am here to enforce the laws of the Republic . . ."

Madame de Dey shuddered.

"Don't you have anything to disclose to me?" he asked.

"Nothing," she answered in surprise.

"Oh, madame," cried the prosecutor, sitting down beside her and changing his tone of voice, "at a time like this, for keeping silent, you or I could be bringing our head to the scaffold. I have observed your character, your soul, and your manners too long to share in the mistake you were able to lead your guests into this evening. You're waiting for your son, I have no doubt of it."

The countess made a gesture of denial; but she had turned pale, and her facial muscles had contracted under her strenuous attempt to wear a deceptive mask of firmness. The implacable eye of the public prosecutor followed each of her movements.

"Very well, receive him," continued the revolutionary official; "but he is not to remain beneath your roof a moment later than seven in th morning. Tomorrow at daybreak, bearing an accusation that I shall get drawn up, I shall come to your house . . ."

She looked at him with a dazed air that would have instilled pity in a tiger.

"I shall demonstrate," he went on softly, "the falsity of the accusation by making a thorough search, and after my report you will be safe from any further suspicions. I shall speak of your patriotic gifts and your civic spirit, and we shall *all* be saved."

Madame de Dey feared some trap; she remained motionless, but her face was burning and her tongue was frozen. The sound of the door knocker echoed through the house.

"Oh!" cried the frightened mother, falling on her knees. "Save him, save him!"

"Yes, let us save him!" replied the public prosecutor, darting a look of passion at her, "even if it should cost *us* our lives."

"I'm undone!" she cried while the prosecutor politely raised her up.

"Ah, madame," he answered, with a fine oratorical flourish, "I wish to owe you to nothing . . . but to yourself."

"Madame, here he . . .!" exclaimed Brigitte, who thought her mistress was alone.

At the sight of the public prosecutor, the old servant, who had been flushed and happy, became motionless and pale.

"Who is it, Brigitte?" asked the official with a gentle, knowing air.

"A conscript that the mayor has sent us to put up," answered the servant, showing the order.

"It's true," said the prosecutor after reading the paper. "We're getting a battalion tonight!"

And he left.

The countess at that moment had too much need to believe in her former procurator's sincerity to form the slightest doubt; she went upstairs swiftly, with barely enough strength to support herself; then she opened the door to the room, saw her son, and dashed into his arms, nearly dead: "Oh, my child, my child!" she cried, sobbing and covering him with kisses that betokened a sort of frenzy.

"Madame!" said the stranger.

"Oh, it's not him!" she cried, recoiling in fright and remaining on her feet in front of the conscript, observing him distraughtly.

"Oh, holy God, what a resemblance!" said Brigitte.

There was a moment of silence, and the stranger himself gave a start at the sight of Madame de Dey.

"Oh, sir," she said, leaning on Brigitte's husband, and at that moment feeling the full force of a sorrow that had almost killed her at its first onslaught; "sir, I can't look at you any longer; permit my servants to take my place and see to your needs."

She went downstairs to her room, half carried by Brigitte and her old servant.

"What, madame!" the housekeeper exclaimed as she sat her mistress down, "is that man going to sleep in Monsieur Auguste's bed, put on Monsieur Auguste's slippers, eat the pâté that I made for Monsieur Auguste! Even if they guillotined me, I . . ."

"Brigitte!" called Madame de Dey.

Brigitte fell silent.

"Be quiet, can't you, you babbler," her husband said to her quietly; "do you want to kill madame?"

At that moment, the conscript made a sound in his room as he sat down at the table.

"I won't stay here," exclaimed Madame de Dey, "I'll go into the hot-house. From there I'll be able to hear better whatever happens outside during the night."

She was still tossed between the fear of having lost her son and the hope of seeing him reappear. The night was terribly silent; there was a frightful moment for the countess when the battalion of conscripts reached town and every man was looking for his quarters there. Her hopes were deceived at every footstep, every sound; soon afterward, nature resumed a terrifying calm. Toward morning, the countess was compelled to go back to her room. Brigitte, who was observing her mistress' movements, not seeing her come out, entered the room and found the countess dead.

"She probably heard that conscript, who's just gotten dressed and who's walking around in Monsieur Auguste's room singing their damned 'Marseillaise' as if he were in a stable!" cried Brigitte. "That's what must have killed her!"

But the countess' death was caused by a deeper emotion, and no doubt by some fearful vision. At the very hour when Madame de Dey died in Carentan, her son was shot by a firing squad in Morbihan. We can add this tragic fact to all those other observations relative to sympathetic thought transference in disregard of the laws of space—documents being assembled with learned curiosity by a few solitary men, which one day will serve to lay the foundations of a new science that has so far lacked a man of genius to formulate it.